CLEAR CREEK JUSTICE

By the same author

Kid Hailer
Montana Rescue
The Trouble With the Law
Easy Target
The Ten Sleep Murders

CLEAR CREEK JUSTICE

BILLY HALL

A Black Horse Western

ROBERT HALE • LONDON

ISBN 0 7090 5940 X

Robert Hale Limited
Clerkenwell House
Clerkenwell Green
London EC1R 0HT

Typeset in Photina by Pitfold Design, Hindhead, Surrey.
Printed and bound in Great Britain by
WBC Book Manufacturers Limited,
Bridgend, Mid-Glamorgan.

ONE

'Kill 'em. 'Cept the girl. I want her.'

The young woman's face blanched, but her chin lifted defiantly. She did not flinch from the dirty outlaw's leer. As his eyes rested on the stretched front of her blouse, the vertical creases at the corners of her mouth deepened. Her lips paled perceptibly, but she said nothing.

A buckskin-clad trapper stood beside her. Furtively he moved his huge hand closer to the spot on his shirt front that gaped open. He, too, said nothing.

A rider watched, unseen, from the edge of the trees. From a short scabbard hanging from the saddle horn, he silently drew a Colt revolving shotgun. He lifted the thong from his holstered pistol and nudged the horse with his heels.

Obediently the horse started forward. It stepped carefully, as though its rider's need for stealth were transmitted through reins or knees, ears pointed alertly at the group in front of them. The man ignored a deer fly, rare at this altitude, that buzzed in his ear. His flat blue eyes bore unflinchingly into the backs of those before him.

A stagecoach had stopped in the road, at the only level spot in a stretch of tortuous climb. The driver, the shotgun guard, and three passengers were standing in a line, their hands in the air. They were faced by four men on horseback, each holding a gun.

The wrinkled stage driver was the first to spot the man approaching from behind the outlaws. His face betrayed nothing. He began to stall for time. 'You got everything we was carryin',' he said. 'You got no call to kill us.'

'That is quite correct!' a corpulent passenger asserted forcefully. 'And it is well worthy of your consideration. Above all, you certainly have no right to abduct the young lady.' His rotund face took on an almost pontifical expression as he continued, 'It is all but a foregone conclusion that if you harm a member of the fairer sex in this country, you will be hunted down and will undergo a sundering of body and soul. Such incorrigible behaviour simply is not tolerated amongst civilized people.'

'What's he sayin', Milt?' one of the horsemen said to the leader, brow furrowed.

'Aw, he's just tryin' to scare us with a bunch of highfalutin' words,' the leader spat. He addressed the meticulously dressed gentleman. 'She's just a whore. Besides, once you're dead, who's going to identify us?'

'Whether she secures her livelihood as a harlot is immaterial,' the man replied, mopping sweat from his forehead and jowls with a white handkerchief. 'She is nevertheless a woman, and as such certainly falls under the protection of the code of the West.'

'Why don't we quit jawin' and get it done?' The words settled like silken petals of poison across the group. The speaker was the smallest of the outlaws. He sat his horse with an eager tension, his eyes shining with anticipation. His finger tightened perceptibly on the trigger, the gun pointing unwaveringly at the bulging stomach of the pompous speaker.

'Don't move! Drop the guns!'

The sharp words cracked like splitting rocks across the stillness of the mountainside. The four gunmen stiffened and paled, as though some unseen hand had wiped the colour from their faces. They all craned over their shoulders at the lone man who had ridden, unheard, to within twenty yards behind them. They looked quickly at each other, realizing he was alone. He couldn't possibly be any match for the four of them, if they acted together.

'Who are you? Why are you buyin' into this?' the leader of the four asked. Gently he nudged his horse to allow him to face his new and unexpected threat.

As he did so, the others followed suit, moving apart slightly to present a more difficult target to the lone, would-be rescuer. As soon as the gunmen began turning away from the inhabitants of the stagecoach, the driver signalled to the others to move to the side, away from the line of fire. As they moved, the driver and the guard moved closer to the guns they had been forced to drop on the ground.

'I said, drop the guns!' the intruder barked.

A barely perceptible move of the smallest man's gun triggered the events that followed too fast to watch. The man moved the revolving shotgun to bear on him and fired in one motion, driving the little man bodily out of the saddle.

Almost instantly the newcomer felt the tug of a bullet at his sleeve and heard the angry buzz of another narrowly missing his ear. The motion of the gun never stopped, however. Three more shots roared so closely together the answering fire of two of the gunmen's pistols were not even heard. Some corner of his mind noted the fourth gunman was already falling when he shot him, but his well-planned motion continued undisturbed. His fourth shot nearly tore the already falling gunman in two.

The stage driver and the guard dived for their guns and rolled to their feet, but there were no live outlaws left for them to face. All four were lying in the rocky and rutted road, motionless in spreading pools of blood.

Time hung in breathless suspension. A magpie called in the distance. A blue jay's scolding from closer among the trees seemed to answer. The horses, whose saddles had been abruptly emptied, sidestepped away from their prone riders, heads tossing nervously.

'That's mighty fast shootin',' the voice of the fifth stage occupant drawled. 'You was on your third one afore I could even get into action.' With one hand he stroked his full, dark beard. His buckskins had the look of expert tanning, and he held a Russian-made .44 in his massive fist. A small wisp of smoke trailed from its barrel.

The lone horseman stared silently at him for a long moment before answering. Finally he said, 'You shouldn't have been able to get any of them, but that one may've gotten me if you hadn't. Where'd you have that hidden, that you could unlimber it that fast?'

The big man shrugged. 'I was waitin' till I thought I had half a chance, but time was gettin' mighty scarce when you showed up. The little guy was plumb anxious to start shootin' folks.'

'You know 'em?'

'I ain't never seen none of 'em before. Have you, Jap?'

The grizzled stage driver shook his head. 'I think I seen the one that was callin' the shots a time or two, down

8

around Ten Sleep. I ain't never seen the others.'

'You headin' for Buffalo?' the newcomer asked.

'Uh huh. I'm Jasper Bursell. Folks call me Jap. That's Shorty Macombe, rides shotgun. We're the regular stage, three days a week each way, Buffalo to Ten Sleep. Say, ain't you that range detective that was hooked up with that hangin' over in Ten Sleep?'

The rescuer's eyes went flat and hard. A screen of steel slammed across emotion that, just for a moment, threatened to expose itself. His broad shoulders stiffened as though against some great unseen force. He dismounted and faced the assembled group. He planted his feet, making his short legs look almost stubby in contrast to his long torso. 'I'm him. Name's Levi Hill.' The words slapped as hard and expressionless as flint. 'You better get these bodies thrown up on top and get on the road.'

The woman and the profusely sweating fat man climbed silently back into the stage. The fat man constantly wiped at his ashen face. The woman only watched with sharp interest as the carnage of battle was removed from the road. The men went through the outlaws' pockets, removing the things stolen from the group and whatever identification they carried, then swung the bodies up to the top of the stage. They lashed them like baggage for the ride over the top and down the steep mountain road. When they finished, the big trapper turned to Levi. He thrust out a hand, then noticed it was bloody, wiped it on his pant leg, then held it out again. 'My name's Charley Johnson. I've heard about the job you had to do down at Ten Sleep. You got my respect. I'd sure be pleased to ride with you a ways, if'n you could stand the company.'

Levi took the extended hand and gripped it briefly. 'I appreciate the offer, but I ain't headin' anyplace in particular.'

'I heard you quit lawin'.'

Levi nodded. 'Got my stomach full.'

Charley nodded in return. 'Got plans for winterin'?'

'Guess not.'

'Well, listen, you might not cotton to offers from a stranger. Your choice. I got me a cabin built along a nice stream that spills into Clear Crick, up above Buffalo. Makin's of a good ranch, some day. I got a trap line strung out that oughta be more'n one man can handle by hisself. If you need a spot to winter, I could sure use the help. We'd go halves on the hides, after expenses.'

Levi was looking the big man over as he talked. 'Why are you riding the stage, then?'

Charley looked embarrassed. He looked off across the tops of the endless evergreens as they carpeted the steepness of the mountainside, then looked back at Levi. 'Fact is, I rode it over to Ten Sleep to watch the hangin'.'

Levi's face turned hard again. His voice was sharply edged with bitterness. 'Just to watch a woman hang! And did you get all the thrill you expected?'

Charley cleared his throat and studied his moccasins. 'Truth is, I didn't go watch after I got there. I ain't never seen a hangin', and I thought I wanted to. When I got there, and it come time, I decided I wasn't that anxious to watch anybody die. Leastways not a woman, and not that way. But, like I said, I sure do admire your guts and your character. A man that does what's right, even when it tears him to pieces, has to be a good man to winter with.'

The silence hung heavily between them until Charley finally broke it again. 'Anyhow, I got good and drunk for a couple days, then waited for my head to quit hurtin' some. Then I hung around over there, drinkin' an' whorin' around for a spell. Finally decided I'd best get back to my own diggin's, so I hopped the stage to head back to Buffalo. My horse and stuff's at the livery barn there.'

'Then I guess you better ride the stage right on back there,' Levi said. He started back towards his horse, standing ground-tied at the edge of the road.

'Naw, I guess not,' Charley drawled. 'I don't mind ridin' that thing up the mountain, but it like to scared me to death goin' down. I reckon I'll ride the big one. Somebody's gotta do it, and it sure beats ridin' that there death-trap down the mountain.'

'I'll tell the sheriff in Buffalo you'll be along with their horses then,' the driver said from his seat atop the stage. He kicked off the brake, snapped the reins, and the six-horse team leaned into the harness.

The young woman leaned to look out of the stage window. Her eyes met Charley's. Levi had been a range detective far too long not to notice something pass wordlessly between them. Then the coach creaked and rocked slowly out of sight up the steep, twisting trail toward the summit.

TWO

Four men had died in two seconds. It was over as swiftly as it had begun. The world settled into the surreal silence. The aftermath of violence has its own aura: the world seems unnaturally still; survivors feel listless, even depressed; the others feel nothing at all.

Levi and Charley watched as the stage team leaned into the harness. The conveyance creaked and bounced over the rocks and along the ruts. The four bodies, lashed on top, rolled back and forth slightly with each twist and bounce. Neither spoke until the stage was nearly out of sight.

'Plumb slow, now,' Charley observed, 'but when Jap gets 'em over the top he'll go down that mountain so danged lickety-split it's a wonder he ever gets there at all. I even promised Glory I'd quit drinkin' and whorin' around if He'd just get me down to Ten Sleep in one piece.'

Levi's eyebrows lifted. 'I thought you said you tied one on in Ten Sleep.'

'Yeah.'

'Promise didn't last long, huh?'

Charley's face colored. He scuffed the dirt with his toe, watching his foot intently. 'Aw, I guess I didn't really mean it when I said it. I reckon He knew it, too. Jap just scared me plumb bad, the way he drove that stage.'

'Knows the mountain, I suppose.'

Charley nodded. 'He does that. I ain't never heard of him wreckin' a stage, but I ain't never gonna ride down with him again if'n I can help it.'

Levi nodded and stepped back into the saddle. Dropping the revolving shotgun into its scabbard, he touched his hat brim to Charley and rode silently into the trees. There was neither sight nor sound to indicate which way he went.

Charley stared after him for several minutes in silence. Shrugging his massive shoulders, he caught up the reins of the outlaws' horses. He stepped into the saddle of the largest and gripping the reins of the other three, he started up the road in the direction the departing stage had gone.

Nearly a mile up the mountain the trail emerged from the trees and began the last leg of the ascent. It was now above timberline. Charley stopped and looked at the rugged slope of rock and red dirt. He wiped the sweat from his brow with his bandanna, stuffing it back into his shirt.

'You going clear to Buffalo tonight?'

Charley jumped so hard he nearly fell from the saddle. He twisted this way and that, trying frantically to find the source of the voice, but seeing nothing. 'Where you at?' he demanded.

Levi moved his horse out of the edge of the timber with a low chuckle. 'You jump like a schoolmom with a garter snake in her desk.'

'Well, what'dya expect?' the trapper demanded. 'You sneak up on a man like a danged Indian and scare the

13

gizzard out of him, then laugh 'cuz he jumps! A man could get shot pullin' somethin' like that!'

'Have to see me before you could shoot me,' Levi observed dryly.

'What you doin' here, anyway?' the trapper asked, the angry edge still tingeing his voice. 'I thought you took off t'other way.'

'Oh, I decided I'd tag along a ways, just to make sure those horses weren't too much for you to handle alone.'

Charley snorted. 'More likely you tagged along to see if I knowed a good campin' spot over on the east slope.'

With one finger Levi pushed his hat brim upward, causing the hat to tilt to the back of his head. A sharp line on his head marked its usual position. Below the line his face was burned brown. Above the line it was an almost ghostly white. 'That did cross my mind,' he grinned. 'I figured you wouldn't be wantin' to go clear to Buffalo without stopping for the night, especially since you like to go down mountains nice and slow.'

'You just never let up, do you?' Charley complained.

'Well, fact is, I ain't had anybody I could talk to for quite a while,' Levi confessed. 'I ain't sure I want to go into trappin', but I thought we could keep each other company for a day or two anyway.'

Charley studied him for a full minute in silence, then nodded. 'Shore be tickled to have your company. 'Sides, three horses is quite a lot to hang on to, all at once.'

'String 'em out, then.'

'What'dya mean?'

Dismounting, Levi shook out the lariat from one of the saddles. He knotted the reins of one horse together, so they couldn't drag, and hooked them over the saddle horn. Then he tied the end of the lariat in the bit ring. Measuring off a proper amount of rope, he tied the lariat to the second horse's saddle horn. He knotted the reins of that horse over the saddle horn as he had the first. Using two lariat ropes, he lashed the three horses together in single file, taking a dally around his own saddle horn with the loose end.

'Now they can string out single file behind us,' he explained to the bemused trapper, 'just like pack horses.'

'Now why didn't I think of that?' the trapper marveled.

'Must have come from Ohio,' Levi responded, with that same twinkle returning to his eye.

'South end o' Illinois,' Charley corrected. 'But I been in this country nigh on to ten years. I just ain't never led a string o' saddled horses nowheres.'

'Where'd you learn to handle a gun like you do?'

'Just practised. When I come out here I was just outa the war. Illinois regiment. This here was a mighty rough country, and me not outa my teens. I figured the one thing that'd keep me alive was knowin' how to shuck a gun in a hurry and shoot straight, so I just spent a whole lot of time practisin'.'

They rode in relative silence up and across the switchbacks of the rock-strewn pass, then down the other side until the trail was again shrouded in timber. Charley turned off the road where a small stream rippled across the rocks, following it up a narrow canyon. About a half-mile from the road there was a steep cliff rising from the edge of the stream. A huge depression had been hollowed out of the vertical wall by countless years of storm and wind.

'Makes a perfect campsite,' Charley explained. 'Stays bone dry, even in a downpour. Lots of deadwood in all directions. Nobody can get near without making enough noise to wake the dead. Fresh water. Good grass for the horses.'

Levi nodded approvingly, and set about picketing the horses for the night. By the time he returned to the campsite, Charley had a small fire going and supper cooking.

After they had eaten, Charley fished out an old, long-stemmed pipe. He filled it, lit it, and leaned back against the rock. Levi filled his coffee mug and moved to the other side of the fire. He was always careful not to stare into the flames, lest he be unable to see into the darkness.

Nearly an hour of silence followed. Finally Charley broke it. 'Pretty nasty business, I reckon, wasn't it?'

Levi didn't bother to ask what he made reference to. He had known he would have to talk about it. He didn't want to. Even as he insisted, in his mind, that he didn't want to, he knew he needed to talk it out. His life had been ripped apart. He had been forced to do things he could never have even imagined and it haunted him without let up.

'Hear the wind in the tops of the pines?' he asked.

Silently, Charley arched his brows, waiting.

'At night, when I'm alone, the wind whispers her name up there. Then I remember what it was like to hold her, and have her tell me how much she loved me. Then the wind changes to a wail that sends shivers clear through my soul. That hangin' didn't just end forever any chance she could be mine: that hangin' ended my life. Every time I hear the wind in the pines I die again. I see her eyes all the time, lookin' and lookin' at me, beggin' for help, then lookin' so awful when they run her horse out from under her. She asked me, every way a woman can ask, to get her out of there and go away with her. I guess I planned to, too. Right up to the time they hung her, I planned to try to get her free and run with her. But I couldn't. I'm a lawman, or I was. I swore I'd uphold the law. And she'd

16

killed a lot of men. No matter how much I loved her, I just couldn't do what she wanted me to.'

Charley puffed his pipe in silence, watching his new-found friend, feeling the agony of his pain, powerless to reach beyond the barrier of his broken heart to help. For thirty minutes they sat in silence.

'So now what?' Charley asked gently, at last.

Levi sighed heavily, and stirred himself to refill his mug from the coffee pot on the edges of the fire's embers. He sat back down and sipped the thick, black brew thoughtfully. 'I turned in my badge and left. I got enough saved up to drift awhile, I guess.'

'The offer of a trappin' partner is still open,' Charley said softly. Then he added quickly, 'I wouldn't be doin' you no favors. It's a rough life up in these mountains in the winter. The traps gotta be tended, whether it's nice out or a blizzard. I won't leave animals to suffer in a trap 'cause I don't want to get cold checkin' the lines. Treatin' hides is dirty, stinkin', hard work. It pays right good, if it's a good year, but you earn every cent of it.'

Levi wordlessly dumped out the grounds from the bottom of his coffee and shook out his bedroll. He rolled his coat for a pillow and put his gun beneath it, then rolled into his blankets. 'I'll give it some thought,' he said. 'Anyway, I'm sorry I unloaded all that on you. Man ought to keep his troubles to himself.'

Charley shook his head. 'Can't agree with that,' he said. 'I seen it in the war. That war ruined and twisted almost every man what fought in it, one way or another. Seein' so many die changes ya. Even worse is havin' to look men in the eye and shoot 'em, an' then tomorrow do it again. An' you know they got a wife or a sweetheart or a mother somewheres, prayin' fer 'em to come home safe. But you got to kill 'em. It does somethin' to a man's soul. You keep all that to yourself, it's like a boil that just keeps festerin' bigger n' sorer. You got to let it bust out, and get it on the outside, so's to let it heal. Man's gotta have somebody to talk to, to do that.'

Levi looked silently into the darkness for a long moment, then nodded once. 'Could be,' he said.

He turned his back to the small fire and slipped into his first sound sleep in a long and painful time.

THREE

Daylight filtered softly into the deep canyon. The high walls would not allow the sharp edges of sunlight to reach the canyon floor for another two hours. The absence of any breeze lent an unearthly silence. A thin fog added to the serenity of the scene.

The two men worked beside the small fire, the only sound the soft clinking of utensils as they readied breakfast. Speaking softly, as though reluctant to break the dream-like aura of the morning, one said, 'I'll go catch us a couple trout for breakfast.'

He returned in less than thirty minutes with four nice trout, cleaned and washed in the stream. His partner had a skillet already on the fire. Wordlessly he rolled the fish in flour and dropped them in the sizzling grease.

'Nice trout,' the huge man with the beard commented.

'They were hungry this morning,' Levi responded. 'They acted like they hadn't seen a worm all summer.'

'Been eatin' them freshwater shrimp, mostly,' the other responded. 'See how orange the meat is? That shore does

19

make 'em tasty.'

As he talked he used a strong stick to fish a Dutch oven out of the coals, and lifted the lid. The smell of freshly baked biscuits wafted into the morning mist, wrenching a twinge of anticipation from Levi's stomach.

'You make biscuits like that all the time?' Levi asked. 'Man cooks like that oughta make some woman a fine wife.'

Charley grunted something unintelligible. He stuffed his mouth with the sweet meat of freshly caught trout and hot biscuits. Both ate in silence until the food was completely gone and they were on their second cup of coffee.

'How far to Buffalo?' Levi asked finally.

''Bout five, six hours,' Charley responded. 'Road's plumb good a-horseback. Ain't bad with a wagon, for that matter, long's you don't have to ride with Jap drivin'.'

Charley began to wash up their dishes and pack their gear. Levi picked up his lariat and went to bring in the horses. He saddled all five, that being the easiest way to haul the saddles and gear from the dead outlaws. They strung out, riding at a fast trot back to the main road, then slowing to a walk as they began the long and crooked descent from high on Powder River Pass, in the Big Horn Mountains.

They rode in silence, walking the horses in the steep descents, and nudging them to a trot along the level stretches. The thin air gave the sun uninhibited power whenever they were out of the timber. They steadily mopped sweat from their eyebrows with their sleeves.

They were walking the horses carefully down a particularly steep stretch of the grade, leaning back in their saddles as far as they could, when Charley yelled back over his shoulder at Levi. 'Somebody's wrecked a wagon!'

They quickened their pace as much as they dared. Levi

stood in his stirrups to see what Charley pointed at. Just below a particularly sharp bend in the steep trail, a wagon lay in the creek bottom, on its side and badly broken. Pieces of wagon and its contents were scattered widely. The team, a fine pair of matched percherons, were still securely in harness. One was lying on his side, tangled in the doubletree, struggling feebly, his nostrils flaring and his eyes rolling wildly. The hind leg that was tangled in the doubletree was bent off at an erratic angle.

The other horse was on his feet, but could not completely straighten his back leg because of the harness attached to the shattered wagon. He appeared to be crouching to leap, two hind legs quivering with fatigue from standing in that forced position.

Tying their horses to a stunted cedar growing at the trail's edge, Levi and Charley scrambled down the rock-strewn slope to the wreck. With his razor-sharp knife, Levi slashed the traces holding the upright horse which straightened its back legs with obvious relief. Levi led him a little way away, watching him closely as he walked. Satisfied he was not seriously hurt, he looped his rein over a tree branch and turned to the other horse. His eyes took in the horse's critical condition and the position of the leg that was obviously badly broken. Grimly he drew his .45. In his mind he drew an X on the horse's forehead, from left ear to right eye, and from right ear to left eye. Where the two lines crossed he fired a single bullet. The horse gave a convulsive shudder and lay still.

Charley yelled from the brush side beside the creek, 'Driver's over here!'

Levi ran to the sound of the other's voice, and found him bent over the still form of a young man. There were no obvious signs of injury. 'He OK?' he asked as he ran up.

Charley shook his head. 'I reckon he drowned. He was face down in the crick, cold as stone. I 'spect he hit his head and was knocked out. Got a pretty good knot on it. His face was in the water. He just lay there an' drowned.'

Levi took off his hat, staring silently at the unknown victim of the accident. 'Brakes busted,' he observed quietly. 'I saw the chock off one of the brakes up on the road. It must have busted, then he couldn't control it or keep it off the team coming down that steep grade.'

They stood in silence, staring at the dead man for nearly a minute, then Levi's head snapped up. 'Listen!' he hissed.

They both stood with their heads tilted sideways, listening intently, for several moments. Then the sound Levi had heard came again. It sounded like a low moan, from the direction the wagon had come as it careered down the mountainside. Both men lunged in that direction.

Urgently they climbed up the slope until they caught a glimpse of calico between a rock and a scruffy clump of sage brush clinging to the slope. As they climbed nearer they could see bare legs and a pair of rough boots that looked out of place on the trim and shapely limbs. Heaving himself up over the last rock, Levi stopped cold.

Lying in a pocket of rocks was the form of a young woman. She was breathtakingly beautiful. Her dress was flung up across her body, exposing most of her legs. They were perfectly formed, marred only by scrapes and bruises that were obviously fresh. Her flaming red hair was spread out across a rock, framing a set of perfect features. A faint bridge of freckles connected her cheeks across the nose. One arm lay at her side. The other was beneath her.

Levi stood as if transfixed, and Charley huffed up beside him. They both stood there, frightened by the pallor of her skin and embarrassed by the exposure of her legs. They looked at each other, and both swallowed hard, as though activated by the same set of reflexes.

Finally Levi climbed over the last rock and leaned over, gently pulling her dress down over the alluring perfection of her legs. Then he lifted her head gently from the rock, sliding his hand beneath it. 'Ma'am?' he said softly. 'Ma'am, can you hear me?'

She moaned softly and stirred slightly. Levi spoke over his shoulder. 'She's got an awful lump on the back of her head. Help me move her enough to get that other arm out from under.'

Charley stirred himself from his trance and climbed into the fissure with them. He lifted the girl's left side gently as Levi took the arm in both hands, moving it out from under the weight of her body. As Charley lowered her back to her previous position, Levi gingerly tested the arm.

'I think it's got one bone busted,' he speculated. 'That's all the bad hurts I can see, except that knot on the head.'

The girl moaned again. 'Best get her some water,' Levi suggested.

'I'll get it,' Charley said, clambering at once out of the defile and starting up the hill to their horses on the road. By the time he returned, the girl had opened stunningly green eyes, and was staring in obvious confusion.

Levi held the canteen to her lips and she took a small sip, then choked. She took another small drink, then looked around in sudden and frightened realization. 'David!' she said, eyes widening as she remembered how she came to be where she was. 'David? Is David all right? Where's David?'

Levi and Charley exchanged a look, and looked back at the girl. She tried to grab Levi's arm, then winced and her eyes glazed with pain as she moved the fractured limb. She recovered almost at once, however, and her eyes turned to

Levi imploringly. 'Where's David?' she demanded again.

Levi cleared his throat. 'Ma'am, I'm . . . I'm just plumb sorry. I'd give most anything not to have to tell you this. Ma'am, it looks like he hit his head, same as you did, but he ended up in the crick, and . . . and, well, ma'am, I'm just plumb sorry.'

Her forehead furrowed into a row of deep creases and tears began to spill from her eyes. She stared at Levi, trying with her eyes to force him to take back the words. He returned her stare wordlessly. A lone tear escaped his own eye, forming a rivulet down across the dust of his cheek. Without really knowing what he was doing or why, he reached out and slid his arms around the girl's shoulders. He gathered her against himself. Her good arm locked around him as she buried her face in his shoulder, sobbing uncontrollably.

Levi held her that way for several minutes, until her sobs subsided. His hand unconsciously stroked the burnished gold of her hair. He struggled in vain for words – any words that would ease her agony. There were none. All the while, Charley nervously studied the rocks, the trees, the fragments of the wagon, and everything else that avoided the pain of the scene before him. When the girl pulled back from Levi, he cleared his throat. 'I reckon we'd best figure out some way to tote your man on down to town, ma'am, and get you to a doctor. That arm needs looking after.'

'I . . . I want to see him,' the girl sobbed in short bursts. 'We . . . we've only been married six months. We just homesteaded about twenty miles south of Buffalo, where . . . where Middle Fork comes down. We . . . we were over to see his brother and his wife. They have a new baby. We were coming home.'

She broke off and started to climb painfully out of the

24

crevice in which she had come to rest. Levi slipped an arm around her waist to balance and help her. He kept her from falling as they slipped and slid down the hill to where her husband still lay beside the North Fork of Clear Creek.

Wordlessly, she stopped beside him, then dropped to her knees. She reached out a trembling hand and brushed the wet, clinging hair from his ice-cold face and forehead. She let her fingers trail across his cheek as her arm dropped. A single sob racked her shoulders but she instantly asserted the force of her will against the tears. She stood, looking pale and many years older than she had moments before.

'There's blankets that were in the wagon,' she said in a flat voice so soft the men could scarcely hear her. 'Please wrap him in one of them, and put him on Ron. The horses are Perch and Ron. Did you shoot Perch?'

'Yes ma'am,' Levi replied. 'His hind leg was broken and he was hurt real bad. I put him out of his misery.'

'Thank you,' she said, in the same distant voice. 'Do you have an extra horse? I can ride with David if you don't.'

'No need for that,' Charley put in, a little too hastily. 'We got three extra horses we're takin' down to Buffalo. Levi, help the lady up the hill. I'll wrap this feller up and get him on his horse. We'll work downstream to find a spot the horse can climb back up to the road.'

Levi gently put his arm back around the girl's waist, urging her away from the body. One more sob nearly broke the surface of her fierce calm as she turned away to start the climb, but she stubbornly refused to allow it any avenue of escape.

She is one tough woman, Levi thought silently.

FOUR

It was a long and painful climb. Her world had fallen apart. Her husband was dead. Still, she made no sound of complaint. She would not be weak!

With a piece of cloth that had been strewn by the wreck, Levi bound her broken arm tightly to her body. With his arm around her, and her good right arm clinging to him, they eventually made their way back up to the tethered horses.

'You need to rest a while before we start?' Levi asked gently when they had reached the shade beside the mounts.

She shook her head quickly, jaws clamped tightly together, making no sound. Levi motioned to a horse and helped her climb into the saddle. He adjusted the stirrups to fit the length of her legs and tried, mostly without success, to keep from admiring those shapely legs so close in front of him as he did so. Mounting his own horse, he picked up the lead rope of the others and they moved out.

It was nearly two miles before the trail leveled off beside

the creek again. Charley was waiting for them in the shade of a spruce tree growing out of solid rock. The percheron with its tragic burden stood stolidly beside him.

The girl looked quickly at the wrapped body, then looked away just as quickly, biting her lower lip. Without a word Charley mounted, and they resumed their sombre journey.

It was nearly dark when they rode into Buffalo. Levi had moved to a position beside the girl to catch her if she fell. Several times she had swayed in the saddle as though she would, but each time she grimly grasped the saddle horn and straightened. They rode straight to the hotel.

Levi dismounted and reached for the girl. She started to dismount on her own, then collapsed, falling into his outstretched arms. He held her against himself until she was able to stand, then stepped back, one hand still clinging to her good arm to prevent her falling.

'Ma'am, I didn't ask your name,' he said. 'I'm Levi Hill. That's Charley Johnson.'

'I'm sorry,' the girl murmured absently. 'I'm Harriet Nelson. They call me Hattie. I . . . I don't have money to stay at the hotel. I . . . I'm not sure David has much money with him, either. I have a friend who lives in town. Can you take me there?'

'If you'd rather,' Levi said at once. 'If you need, we'll foot the bill at the hotel, but it'd be better if you were with friends. Is it too far to walk?'

'It's . . . it's down the street a ways. I think I need to walk, if you'll come with me. Please?'

'Sure,' Levi said, a little embarrassed. 'Charley, I'll go ahead and take her there, and put the horses in the livery barn. You could take, uh, David . . . to the undertaker, then get us a room at the hotel, I suppose.'

'Shore,' Charley agreed. 'I'll likely be over at the Pastime

27

when you get back.'

Levi looked the way Charley tilted his nose, and saw the bright lights across the street. The sign on the front boasted, Pastime Liquor And Pleasure Emporium. He nodded wordlessly, and placed one hand gingerly on Hattie's right elbow to steady her.

In a matter of thirty minutes he had escorted the girl safely to the stunned but sympathetic arms of the Miller family. He stabled the horses at the livery barn, and walked back up the street. He looked at the hotel, then decided it was unlikely Charley would be there, and started for the saloon.

He was four steps short of the door when a squirming mass of men erupted through it, cascading into the street. With a roar, Charley gained his feet and sent one of his assailants backward with a crashing blow of his huge fist.

As he did, two others caught him simultaneously in the wind with theirs. He grunted as he doubled forward. Each of the men grabbed one of his arms. A third grabbed a handful of hair from behind. Between the three of them, they were able to hold the huge man, even though his heaving strength kept them sliding back and forth as they fought to contain the mighty arms.

The one he had caught squarely still lay in the street, motionless. A fifth man approached slowly, a grin playing at the corners of his mouth. 'You picked on the wrong bunch this time, you stinkin' hide-scraper. Nobody messes around with the Pucketts!'

He stepped forward and swung with all his strength, smashing his fist into Charley's nose while his brother held Charley's head motionless, and the others held his arms.

As the blood flew in all directions, he drew back to swing again, but was jerked off balance by someone gripping his cocked fist. Cursing, he whirled to face the intruder, and Levi looped a sweeping blow into the middle of his stomach. As the surprised assailant doubled forward, Levi put a hand on the back of his head and lifted his knee into the man's face, feeling the bones of his nose and cheeks crunch. He followed at once with a short right hook into the side of the man's jaw, sending him to the dirt like a clubbed ox.

With a roar Charley flung the distracted pair gripping his arms away. He chopped an elbow backward into the one grasping his hair. The man grunted and released his grip, leaving Charley free to join his friend in the fray.

The two fought like cornered wildcats, taking and receiving innumerable blows as a crowd gathered on the sidewalk. One by one the Puckett brothers fell to the ground, until Levi was left fighting with the one remaining antagonist.

The brother that had been felled in the beginning by Charley had recovered and rejoined the fight, only to be knocked out again. The one Levi was struggling with was the biggest of the lot, nearly as big as Charley. Levi hit him again and again, until his face resembled chopped beef steak, but he could not bring the man down. His massive fists had connected several times as well, and Levi's eyes were beginning to close with the swelling around them. He knew he had to do something quickly.

The man he faced sensed his desperation and lunged forward, arms outstretched to try to catch Levi in a grip that would allow him to utilize his superior strength. Levi sidestepped, but not quite far enough, and the man's right hand grasped his shirt front. Instead of trying to jerk away, Levi lunged forward, driving his head into the bigger man's face as he drove both fists, with all his strength, into his midsection. The man grunted and loosened the grip on

Levi's shirt front.

As he felt the grip loosen, Levi spun, twisting the shirt free of the grip, then continued his spin, bringing his upraised right boot sharply into the big man's jaw. The foot connected with jarring force. The man cartwheeled to the dirt where he lay in a crumpled mass. Levi looked around quickly to see if there was any further threat, but all five brothers lay motionless in the street. He started to grin at Charley, but a cold voice cut like a knife of doom through the gathering darkness.

'That's the end of that! Turn around.'

Levi and Charley both turned slowly to face a sixth man they hadn't even seen. 'Lige Puckett!' Charley breathed.

Levi sized up the newcomer. He was smooth shaven, where the others all wore beards; his clothes were well fitting and tailor-made, where theirs were rough homespun; he wore twin holsters, tied down and each hand held an elaborately engraved, silver-plated, pearl-handled, Colt .44.

'Didn't you hear Zach say it wasn't smart to mess with the Pucketts?' he snarled. 'You two should've listened.'

A gun roared and a hole appeared as if by magic in the gunman's chest. It was followed by a second, two inches to the right of it, before the roar of the first shot faded. A look of stunned surprise crossed Lige's face. He stared down in disbelief at the front of his shirt. His eyes lifted to the gun he hadn't even seen leap into Levi's hand, then continue upward to Levi's face.

'How'd . . . how'd you do . . . do that?' he whispered. His guns grew too heavy to hold and fell from his grip. Still staring fixedly into Levi's face, he fell slowly forward and lay still.

Charley looked just as stunned. 'How in Sam Hill did

you do that?' he breathed. 'He was holdin' down right on you! He didn't never even see you move! That there just ain't possible! They ain't nobody fast enough to draw and shoot a man what's holdin' a gun on him!'

The crowd that had been standing in stunned surprise exploded in a sudden gaggle of wonderment. Levi holstered his gun and turned away. He walked slowly and painfully toward the hotel, with Charley hurrying to catch up.

They said nothing until they were in their hotel room and had washed up, rinsing blood out of their clothes and off their bodies. They patched up their cuts and scrapes and bruises, then Charley resurrected the subject.

'How'd you do that, Levi? I thought we was dead for certain.'

'He'd have killed us, all right,' Levi agreed. 'The trouble is, most people don't know it takes less time to draw and shoot than it does to react to what someone else does. He wasn't expecting me to draw against him, and he wasn't ready to shoot us till he'd talked himself up to it. By the time he could see what I was doing and react to it, he was already shot.'

Charley mulled over the idea in silence for a while, then said, 'Fastest thing I ever heard tell of. They'll be talkin' 'bout that around here for ten years! I don't reckon we've heard the last of them, though. Lige – I think his real name was Elijah – was the fastest gun in the outfit, but there's eight of them Puckett boys. Well, seven now. They've still got all the bark on, and they stick together like glue.'

'What started it?'

'Aw, they was pickin' on Liz somethin' awful.'

'That whore on the stage?'

'Uh, yeah. But listen, she ain't nothin' like all the other whores! That there is one mighty fine little gal. I ain't

noways sure how she come to be a whore, but she's
different. Choosy too. She didn't want the Pucketts'
business. That's what started 'em in on her.'

'You got me in a fight over a whore?' Levi asked again.

Charley looked embarrassed, but belligerent. 'Like I told
you, she ain't like them others,' he insisted. 'I sorta like
that little ol' girl.'

Levi shook his head in disbelief, but said nothing more.
A familiar cold wind blew up the length of his spine. He felt
the unmistakable premonition of impending trouble
overshadow him. It hovered there so strongly he forgot, for
a little while, the weight of the grief he could never leave
behind.

FIVE

'Hill? I am Sheriff Angus. Sure an' I'll be needin' to talk to you.'

Levi eased the door opened and stepped back, keeping his hand on his gun until he saw the badge on the big man's chest. He relaxed as the sheriff stepped into the room, eyes darting quickly around its interior. 'Morning, Sheriff. You're out and about early.'

The early morning sun slanting through the window made the sheriff's hair and moustache even redder than it normally appeared, if that were possible. His pale-blue eyes took in every aspect of Levi's appearance as he answered, holding out his hand.

'The name is W.E. Angus,' he said, as Levi lost his hand in the immensity of the man's grip. 'Folks call me Red. Sure and I never understood why. I hear you had a mite bit of trouble when you rode in last night.'

Levi returned the careful study of the man as he formed his answer. Real outbreak of redheads around here, he told himself silently, remembering the woman they had rescued from the wagon wreck the day before. The white of the sheriff's forehead above his hat line was so mottled with freckles it looked almost comical.

He liked the open honesty reflected in the sheriff's face. 'Lot more trouble than I wanted, that's for sure,' he responded. 'I'm not sure I'd have even bought into the scrap if I'd known it was over a whore.'

The sheriff's eyebrows shot up. His moustache seemed to bristle. 'You mean you're tellin' me you'd have let the Pucketts beat a man to death because you didn't agree with what started the fight?'

Levi's eyes whipped up to the sheriff's. 'I didn't say that! It galls me sore, though, that I had to shoot a man over a whore.'

'That you had to shoot the man, I'm forced to agree,' the sheriff answered, eyes boring into Levi. 'But I'm bein' a bit troubled by your attitude. It's seemin' to me yourself killed the man to keep you from gettin' killed.'

'Sounds like you've already been checking things out,' Levi observed.

The sheriff nodded. 'I've been talkin' to some that was there, and I've sent some telegrams this mornin' and I've been checkin' up on you some, 'tis true. Seems my duty, you see. When a man comes into my town and right off kills a man, I ought to know somethin' about him. When the man he kills is a known gunman who's kept half the town scared ever since we finished that thing out at the T-Bar-A, I'm even more interested.'

'He obviously intended to kill me and Charley both,' Levi inserted into the sheriff's monologue.

'Sure, I'm knowin' the truth of that. Like I say, I did my checkin' before I came to talk to you. But I'm a bit curious,

I am. What is it that you have against whores? If me information is right, you saved the life of the very whore we're talkin' of not two days ago.'

'I got no time for them is all,' Levi answered. 'I was raised to believe the way they make their living is wrong. I've been a lawman long enough to know they cause trouble everywhere they go. I personally think they ought not be allowed in a town. I sure wouldn't lower myself to fighting over a woman any man can have by forking over his two dollars.'

'Well now, ain't you bein' the righteous one!' the sheriff chuckled. 'I'll tell you what, Hill; I think it's a mistake to pickle all whores in the same barrel, just as it is to say all lawmen are alike. 'Tis true for a fact that most of the whores are a bad lot. Some of 'em took to the life 'cause they like men. More of 'em, seems to me, 'cause they hate men. But I've known some that was on the line for a lot of other reasons, and a good one or two I've known, in spite of the way they make their livin'. I even knew one that married a man, once. Made him a real fine wife, she did. Now, I don't do business with 'em, and wouldn't if they was free. I'm a Christian and a family man, but I try not to be judgin' too strong neither.'

Levi returned the sheriff's stare for several heartbeats before he answered. Finally he said, 'Did you come callin' this morning just to share your philosophy about whores?'

The sheriff started to say something, then stopped himself. He sighed, and said, 'Seems to me you're the one brought up the subject. I came here to get your version of what happened last night.'

'Not much to tell,' Levi said. 'When I came back from taking the young lady who lost her husband – Hattie Nelson, I think her name is – to her friends' house – the

Millers – and put up the horses from the bunch who tried to rob the stage – you heard all about that, you said?' The sheriff only nodded, so he continued, 'Well, when I was coming back up the street, Charley and three of them other fellas come rollin' outa the Pastime. The three of them got a'hold of him for the fourth to work over, and he was gettin' started pretty good. I just bought in to even up the odds a little, and we sorta cleaned house on what turned out to be five of them. Then this other one – Elijah, I think – threw down on us from behind, and meant to kill us both, so I shot him.'

'Just like that? He's holdin' two guns on you, fixin' to send the banshees for your lost soul, so you just decides to shoot him. And how, I'm wantin' to know, can a man be gettin' his gun out fast enough to do that?'

Levi shrugged. 'Just takes a man longer to react than it does for a fast man to draw and shoot.'

The sheriff digested that statement for a few seconds, then said, 'Well, I got a feelin' in me middle that says we ain't done with this deal yet. Now, why don't you go back and be startin' at the beginning. I'm needin' to know how you found the hold up of the stage, and everything that happened from there till you made the holes that was letting the Devil out of Lige. He's one gunman I've been getting some worried about how I was going to handle, but like I said, he's got seven brothers we ain't likely bein' all done with.'

Levi thought for just a moment, then responded. 'If I'm going to have to do that much talking, maybe we'd ought to go down to the dining-room. I may need some nourishment to talk that long.'

The sheriff chuckled. 'Fair enough. Sure and you've stirred up more excitement in two days than we've had to deal with in the past two months. Instead of the dining-room, though, let's be crossin' over to Rita Henson's. She's having better food than the hotel, and it's a wee bit cheaper, to boot.'

An hour later the two came out of Rita's Café and went in separate directions. As Levi started across the street to the hotel, he saw Charley coming out of the Pastime. He stopped to wait for him. 'Drinkin' this early in the day?'

'Naw,' Charley responded. 'I just took Liz over to Louie's for breakfast.'

'Food's really good at Rita's,' Levi observed.

Charley looked at his boots as he scuffed the dirt of the street. 'Rita, she won't serve the girls from the Pastime at her place. Louie's ain't as good for food, but it beats what the bar sets out.'

'Sheriff talk to you?'

'Uh huh. Red's a good man. He got in as sheriff when Canton went over to the big ranchers and hired out to do their killin' for 'em. It was Red what got the posse together that stopped all the hired guns of the Cattlemen's Association, out at the T-Bar-A that time.'

Levi nodded his head, indicating he knew the story. He said only, 'The Johnson County War.'

'Yup. Red Angus shore had his hands full with that one.'

'Seems like a good Irishman.'

'You thought any more about throwin' in with me?'

In fact Levi had thought a great deal about it in the past couple of days. He had turned the matter over and over in his mind during the past night, unable to sleep. He had no place to go. His family, his real family, were dead long ago. As a child he had hidden in a clump of sage and watched them massacred by Indians. The family that took him in had been good to him. It was on a quest to rescue their daughter from a band of renegade Crows that he had decided on a career as a lawman. He had ridden as a Pinkerton Range Detective until the deal at Ten Sleep.

Now he had no job at all. He could do a lot worse than team up with Charley and trap all winter. In the spring, with a good chunk of money in his pocket from the winter's furs, he would be in a much better position to plan his future. Now the pain in his heart was much too fresh to allow him to think clearly beyond the immediate.

'Yeah,' he said, after a long pause. 'I guess I got nothin' better to do. I'd be happy to winter with you.'

Charley let out a whoop and slapped Levi on the back, nearly sending him sprawling to the street. 'I got an order already turned in at Thompson's General Store for supplies,' he said. 'I reckon there'll be nigh a hundred dollars' worth. You got money enough to go halves on 'em?'

Levi nodded absently. 'You have a way to get them up to your cabin?'

'Got a couple pack mules and my horse at the livery barn. I'll meet you at the general store in two hours, and we'll pack up and ride out.'

Levi nodded, and crossed the rest of the way to the hotel. He crossed the lobby and had his foot on the bottom step, when a soft voice stopped him.

'Mr Hill? May I talk with you for a minute?'

He turned to see Hattie Nelson and another young woman about her age just rising from two of the lobby's chairs. The redness around her eyes seemed to clash with the red of her hair. The deep clear green of those eyes contrasted sharply with the pallor of her skin, but she was calm and composed. Her left arm was in a sling bound tightly against her. A large bruise discolored one cheekbone. There was a bandage on her good arm. She spoke softly, but her voice was strong and controlled. 'Mr Hill, I wanted to stop over to thank you for saving my life, and for taking care of David. You were very considerate. I appreciate it a great deal.'

At a loss for words, Levi studied the hat in his hands for an awkward moment. 'Well, ma'am, I'm sure sorry about your husband. Do you have any idea what you're going to do now?'

Her eyes threatened to fill and spill over, but did not. She shook her head. 'I'm really not thinking clearly enough yet to make any long-range plans. Becky and Tom have asked me to stay with them for a while. Oh, I'm so sorry! I've completely forgotten my manners. Becky, this is Mr Levi Hill. Mr Hill, this is Rebecca Miller.'

'Uh, yes, ma'am. We met last night, when I took you over there.'

'Oh. Of course. I'm sorry. I'm afraid I don't remember last night too clearly. The doctor came over to their house and set my arm and things. I was just afraid you might leave town before I had a chance to thank you, so I came over right away this morning.'

'You sure don't have to thank me,' Levi said, feeling even as he said it that it sounded foolish and empty, but he couldn't get hold of any other words to say.

'We must get back to the house,' Hattie continued. 'I have much more to get done than I feel like doing, but I suppose the activity is probably good for me. Goodbye, Mr Hill.'

'Goodbye, ma'am.'

'Please call me Hattie.'

'Yes ma'am. I mean . . . Hattie. Goodbye.'

He watched the two women walk away, fascinated by the play of the morning light on Hattie's hair as the soft breeze stirred it. He stood without moving until they were out of the front door and gone from sight.

SIX

A cold wind of premonition kept rippling up and down Levi's spine. When he was a range detective, he almost welcomed that feeling; it meant coming to grips with a case, facing a danger, solving a mystery. Now it only meant trouble. He didn't want trouble. He wanted only to be left alone, to be allowed to bury himself in his own grief.

Eager to get out of town, he retrieved his horse from the livery barn, packed his things in his bedroll and saddlebags, and went to the general store. Charley was just finishing. Both pack mules were fully loaded, their loads covered with tarpaulin. He was weaving a complicated pattern of knots over the load with a rope, fastening them securely to the mules.

'Know how to throw a diamond hitch?' he greeted Levi.

'Nope. Always wondered how. I've seen freighters and prospectors use it, but never could figure it out.'

'Here. I'll show you.'

Over the next fifteen minutes Charley taught Levi the intricate knot. He watched as Levi tied and retied the mules' burden until the diamond-shaped spaces, framed by rope, were evenly distributed and equal in size.

All the while they worked, he kept watch up and down the bustling street. He glanced frequently at the upstairs windows, watching for any movement that would ring bells of alarm in his mind. He knew the sheriff was right; they were almost certainly not finished with the Pucketts, but he had seen no sign of any of them this morning.

The morning was half gone when they rode single file out of town, heading south along Clear Creek, following the road. At the edge of town he caught a furtive movement out of the corner of his eye. His gun was in his hand as though of its own volition but all he saw clearly was a boot heel disappearing behind the corner of a building. He watched over his shoulder for a long way, stopping in the edge of timber from time to time, but he could see no indication they were being followed. In spite of that, every time they crossed a long stretch of open ground, the hair on the back of his neck prickled incessantly.

When they came to the confluence of North Fork with the main stream, they turned due west, following the lesser stream up into the mountains.

As they climbed, the country became increasingly beautiful. Scrubby evergreens and sage brush gave way to soaring pines, firs and spruce, interspersed with the dusty green of aspen groves. The dried brown grass of the prairie turned to the lush green of mountain meadows, watered by springs whose seeps were continually dammed and spread by countless beaver. Summer wild flowers bloomed everywhere.

In mid-afternoon they emerged from the timber into a mostly clear valley, three miles long and a mile wide. At the edge of the trees Levi stopped. He stared breathlessly at the panorama of beauty. The floor of the valley was a solid carpet of wild flowers, their blues, reds, yellows and purples blending together in an unbroken profusion of color. Small clumps of aspen quivered in the breeze. The edges of the valley beyond were covered with lush growth of evergreens, showing at least four shades of green. Several sheer cliffs of reddish and tan stone jutted up from the rim of the valley. The blue, snow-capped peaks behind them formed the perfect backdrop to the scene of paradise.

Several small streams meandered across the valley, producing areas of swampy grasses and shallow ponds. In one of those ponds near at hand, a great bull moose lifted his dripping muzzle to study the intruders, then returned nonchalantly to his underwater browsing. Without moving from his tracks, Levi could count half a dozen beaver ponds.

It took Levi fully fifteen minutes to spot the cabin. When he did, it looked as if it had grown there with the trees – as though it had always been there and belonged as completely as the browsing moose.

The cabin stood on a high knoll, framed on three sides by tall trees. It was squarely built and tightly chinked against the severity of mountain winters. Its roof was of hand-hewn shakes, and it had two windows of real glass.

'How'd you get real glass up here in one piece?' was the first comment Levi made.

Charley threw back his head and laughed an exaggerated complaint to the skies. 'Can you beat that? The man just sticks his nose into the nearest thing to Heaven he's ever seen, and he wants to know how I got glass up here! Hauled it up on the mules, I did. Got it up here first try.'

'It's beautiful!'

'What, the glass?'

'No, the valley. It's like something out of a dream!'

'It is. It's been my dream for many a year, afore I found it,' Charley acknowledged. 'I figure it'll support me in a grand way with furs for a few years. Then, when I get the beaver cut down a ways, it'll grow to better grass, and it'll support cattle. It needs a few beaver, to keep the water slowed down a mite, but not so many like it's got now. It ain't as high as a man'd think, either. Winters in this valley ain't nowhere near what they are higher up. With good grass, I can put up plenty hay for a good size herd of cattle to live on all winter. They can summer higher up on open range. It'll make a real fine ranch.'

'It's beautiful!' Levi said again, at a loss for any other way to describe it.

'Don't know why nobody's ever settled in it,' Charley mused. 'It's only about a six-hour ride from town, if'n you ain't packin' heavy. Mite off the beaten path, though.'

'I doubt if the big cattlemen have figured out how good the grass will be here, once the beaver are reduced to reason,' Levi offered.

Charley nodded thoughtfully. 'Could be. Most folks would just see a swampy valley, I 'spect. Even there, though, cows ain't gonna bog down. Ground's too rocky.'

As if to prove the wisdom of his words, an old cow, with a calf trailing close at her side, emerged from the trees and began to graze placidly on the lush grass. 'See that ole mossy-horn?' Charley pointed. 'Neither her nor her calf got any brand at all. There's quite a bunch of 'em. They're strays from two or three generations back. They winter here. I eat as much beef as venison. I got a brand. I figure to start slappin' an iron on some directly.'

'Make you a good start,' Levi agreed absently, still

44

absorbed in the grandeur of the mountain beauty.

Levi felt strangely heavy, as though his eyes had drunk in more beauty than his heart could hold. Even so, he was reluctant to stop drinking in the idyllic scene spread before him. Finally, with a sigh, he lifted his reins and urged his horse to move. Charley and the mules were already wending their way across the valley.

Charley talked busily as they unpacked the mules. 'Got to get us a hide house built first thing,' he said. 'Cabin's already got two bunks. Figgered I might come up with a partner sometime. Lean-to I used for hides last year's shot. Too close to the house anyway. Hides get pretty ripe when the wind's wrong. Gotta get hay put up for the horses and mules, too. Got a mower and a rake and a bucker to rick the stacks. Hauled 'em up here in parts, so's the mules could do the hayin'. They're good workers, them mules are.'

Listening to Charley's excited chatter, Levi sized up the situation. They had two months of intense work before the trapping season began. Fair enough, he said silently. Oughta be work enough to keep me too busy to think.

He braced himself against the intrusion of Ann's face on to his consciousness. He deliberately tried to replace it with the ashen face of Hattie Nelson. He was partially successful, for a moment. He remembered that face, framed by the flaming hair as she had lain among the rocks where he had found her. It was crowded out again almost immediately, however, by the pleading eyes of his lost love.

'Gonna be a long winter,' he muttered.

SEVEN

'Oooh,' Levi gasped as he sat up on the edge of the bunk. 'I thought I was in better shape'n that. I can't hardly move!'

Charley chuckled dryly as he worked his arms back and forth, working the stiffness from his own shoulders. 'That axe will make an old man out of a feller.'

For two days they had been felling trees and snaking the logs to the building site with the mules. They had nearly enough logs to build the hide house needed for their winter's trapping harvest. It was time to begin shaping them and fitting them together.

In the ensuing days the walls took shape quickly. Near noon on Saturday, they surveyed the nearly completed walls. 'Reckon that'll hold 'er till Monday,' Charley observed.

'You don't work on Sunday?' Levi asked, eyebrows raised.

'Nope.'

'Goin' to town?'

'Yup.'

'Goin' to church?'

'Nope. Ain't much of a church-goin' man.'

'Why don't you work on Sunday, then?'

'Well, I figger the Lord knowed what he was doin' when he said a man oughta work six days and rest one. 'Sides, I gotta go to town once in a while. 'Specially when they's a woman I wanta see.'

'That one off the stage, I suppose.'

'Uh huh. You goin' to town?'

'Yeah, I guess I'd just as well. I might even go to church, come tomorrow mornin'.'

'You a church-goer?'

'Every chance I get.'

'Seems odd for a gunman to be a church-goer.'

'Never thought of myself as a gunman. I make a livin' with my gun, but I ain't never been on the off side of the law doin' it. Most of the time it's been with a badge. I never killed a man I didn't have to. I've never had the law after me for anything. Don't guess I ever will.'

'Well, if'n we're gonna get to town afore it gets dark, we'd best be gettin' down to the crick and takin' a bath.'

The westering sun cast the main street of Buffalo in shadow as they rode into town. They brought along a dressed-out deer they'd killed the day before. Levi took it to the back door of Rita's Café, sold it to the cook and split the money with Charley. *Guess my half'll pay for my room and eats while we're in town,* he told himself silently.

He spent the early part of his evening in the Pastime. He drank coffee, to the bartender's disgust, watched the card games, and studied the people who came and went.

Charley spent most of the evening at a table in the rear of the barroom, drinking slowly, talking with the woman from the stage. Several times Levi noticed men approach her, but she only shook her head and went back to her conversation with Charley. She ain't makin' much money for a Saturday night, Levi observed to himself.

After a time he strolled outside and walked the length of main street and back, then entered the hotel and settled down in the lobby. He spent the rest of the evening watching people pass through, or go by the front windows. He went to bed while the town was still strong.

It was nearly morning when he heard the key fumbling in the room lock. He gripped his pistol silently as the door opened and Charley's bulk lurched through. The smell of liquor filled the room. Charley sprawled on the other bed without making any effort to undress. Levi rose and relocked the door, then went back to sleep.

The sun was flooding its brilliance into the room when Levi rose. He watched with amusement as Charley stirred.

'Ain't they some sort of blind for that window,' the big man growled, squinting against the painful rays.

'Sunshine ain't too painful to me,' Levi quipped.

'Yeah, I noticed you was drinkin' up the free coffee.'

'Figured one of us oughta keep a clear head.'

'Glad you was,' Charley responded. 'Did you see that blond feller sittin' at the back table?'

'Uh huh. Looked familiar, but I couldn't place him.'

'Nathan Puckett. One of the ones we whupped up on the other day. If'n we was both hittin' the bottle he'd likely come back with the rest of 'em, but they ain't likely to face us when we're together and one of us is sober.'

As he talked, Charley had filled the wash basin from the large pitcher beside it, washing his eyes and face gingerly.

'I shore don't know how come that stuff tastes so good at night and hurts so much in the mornin',' he complained.

'You should have spent more time upstairs and less time

drinking.'

'Never did go upstairs,' Charley said.

Levi's eyebrows lifted in surprise. 'You serious? I thought that's what you went over there for.'

'Well . . . well I guess I sorta thought so too, only somehow it just didn't seem the thing to do. I just wanted to talk to her, and I guess keep her away from all them other guys. Some of 'em was a-gettin' plumb owly, though, 'cause I was a-hoggin' her all night.'

'I don't suppose the other girls minded the extra business,' Levi responded dryly.

Conversation lulled as the two men dressed. Levi shook out a broadcloth suit he had removed from his bag the night before, draping it across the back of a chair. It was surprisingly free of wrinkles. He carefully donned a lace shirt, topped with a stand-up collar, then put the suit on as Charley watched in surprise.

'You shore do amaze a man,' he breathed.

'Nothin' wrong with bein' civilized,' Levi grinned.

'Next thing I know you'll start spoutin' Latin or Greek or somethin',' the big man complained.

'*Scientia omnibus rebus anteit*,' Levi shot back.

Charley threw up his hands and started for the door. 'I give up! I tole Liz I'd rent a horse from the livery barn and we'd go off fer a ride up in the hills today,' he said as he went out. 'She's packin' a lunch, so I'll meet you back here 'round the middle o' the afternoon, an' we'll light out fer home.'

The door shut behind him without waiting for an answer. Levi stared at its blankness. 'Sounds more like he's courtin' than seein' a whore,' he muttered. 'Sure settin' himself up for a fall.'

He removed his .45 from its holster and thrust it into his

waistband beneath his shirt. 'Still don't seem quite right to pack a gun to church,' he muttered. 'Only thing worse is goin' without it.'

EIGHT

Nobody wore a visible gun. Buffalo had a distinct Sunday feel; businesses were closed; few people were on the street, and those who were, were mostly *en route* to church, on some sort of outing, or off to visit someone.

After breakfast Levi joined those walking toward the white frame church at the northern end of main street. He chose a seat near the back, close to a side window. Almost at once his eyes lit on the Miller family, accompanied by Harriet Nelson.

She was stunning in her black dress, the lace bodice buttoned clear to her chin. Thick curls of flaming hair formed the perfect frame for the breath-taking beauty of her face. Her eyes were still red with the tell-tale marks of her grief, but her face was calm and composed. He returned the nod carefully, then turned his attention to the preacher.

When the service was dismissed he started toward Harriet and the Millers, but his path was blocked by the bulk of a familiar figure. 'Pardon me, my good man, but I have not been presented with the opportunity of properly

51

expressing my appreciation for your heroic actions.'

Levi halted, groaning inwardly as he recognized the portly rider of the stagecoach he had rescued. 'No thanks necessary,' he mumbled, stepping to move around the man.

'Nonsense,' the man rejoined, moving to block Levi's attempted escape. 'Such acts of heroism at such great personal risk must not go unnoticed. I certainly would not have mustered the courage to speak as I did, had I not seen your timely approach from behind those brigands. They would surely have accomplished their expressed intention of dispatching the entire lot of us if you had not intervened. My name is P.T Grossman, headmaster of the school. I am most proud to make your acquaintance, Mr Hill.'

'How'd you know my name?'

'Oh, I have made abundant enquiries into your identity and background. I consider it most fortuitous that Providence placed you in the proper juxtaposition to effect our rescue, and you most certainly were the right man for that Providence to so position. Well, I simply must not tarry further, but please accept my most sincere gratitude and approbation. Oh, Parson, might I discuss with you for a moment your implied nuances of the concept of Christian archives in the light of recently discovered . . . .'

Levi exhaled a sigh of relief and looked back to the spot where the Millers and Harriet had been sitting, but the pews were empty. Feeling a twinge of disappointment, he walked out into the bright sunlight.

'Excuse me, Mr Hill?'

He looked in surprise to find Tom and Rebecca Miller at his elbow. Hattie Nelson sat in a two-seat spring buggy a short way behind them. 'Mr Hill,' Rebecca Miller said again, 'have you made plans for dinner today? We have dinner in the oven at home. We would be most happy to have you join us if you don't have a previous engagement.'

'Why, thank you. I, yes, I mean no, I mean yes. I'd . . . I'd be real happy to join you.'

Rebecca's eyes danced momentarily at his discomfiture, then returned to their somberness, but she said nothing. Tom said, 'Just as well hop up and ride over there with us.'

Levi walked to the buggy and tipped his hat to Hattie.

'Ma'am, I mean, Hattie, it's good to see you out today.'

'I am much too restless to stay at home,' she replied, pulling her dress over to make room for him on the seat. 'I'm glad you're able to come over and eat with us. I was afraid it would be terribly improper for me to ask you, but it really was my idea, and . . .'

'Now, Hattie,' Rebecca scolded gently as Tom boosted her up into the wagon's front seat. 'There is certainly nothing wrong with our inviting Mr Hill home to dinner! It's not as though every man who steps through our door is already trying to court you, you know.'

'But, I don't want anyone to start any kind of talk . . . .'

'How's your arm?' Levi interrupted uncomfortably. 'Your scrapes and bruises seem to be healing up pretty well.'

'It doesn't hurt badly at all any more,' she responded, obviously relieved that he had changed the subject. 'I have some other bruises that actually hurt a lot more than the arm does. I'm really very lucky.'

You're also very beautiful, Levi almost said aloud as he looked into the emerald depths of her eyes.

Her conversation was almost totally of her late husband, the plans they made together, the land they had homesteaded, and her absence of any idea what to do, now that he was dead. Levi offered little, but listened much, encouraging her to talk.

In mid-afternoon Levi and Charley rode out together, heading south on the road back to their secluded valley. Neither spoke, each lost in a world of his own thoughts.

At the edge of town Levi caught a glimpse of a hat disappearing into a sagebrush-lined draw thirty yards from the road. He yelled at Charley and left his horse in a headlong dive into the grass at the edge of the road. He rolled as he landed, coming to his feet without stopping. He darted into a clump of chokecherry bushes, drawing his gun as he did. He turned and saw Charley lying behind a patch of soapweed, his gun also drawn.

They waited without moving for several minutes, but nothing happened. Levi eyed a clump of sage near the edge of a small ravine. He sprinted to it, diving to the ground almost against it. Nothing happened.

Slowly he inched forward until he could see into the ravine. Tracks of a single horse went both directions in the dry dust of the gully's bottom. He slid down into the ditch, and followed the direction of the tracks until he found where the horse had been held.

'What'd you see?' Charley asked, as he walked carefully to the edge of the ravine.

'Just a glimpse of someone in the brush,' Levi responded. 'Found his tracks easy enough, but he's gone. Looks like he was waitin' and watchin' the road for someone. Musta been us, 'cause he sure lit out when I spotted him.'

He showed Charley the marks that tracked the rider to his vantage point at the edge of the ravine, and the cigarette butts that littered the spot where he had waited.

'One of the Pucketts, shore's anything,' Charley growled.

Levi did not disagree. They both rode with heightened alertness until they were well out of town.

The turmoil in Levi's mind persisted. The face of his lost

love kept appearing in the air before him, but almost as persistently the face of Hattie Nelson was there beside it, vying for his attention. He had enjoyed the dinner and the conversation a great deal more than he would have thought possible, and Hattie had brightened noticeably as she talked. It was with difficulty that he had torn himself away to meet Charley so they could return home.

Each time he started to talk to Charley, the furrowed mask of the big man's face warned him back to silence. When they arrived, as though by some prearranged plan each man turned out his horse and grabbed his axe. They chopped and stacked firewood in feverish competition of endurance until darkness engulfed the valley. Only then did they stop, each puffing heavily with his exertion.

'Life shore ain't never easy,' Charley concluded finally. It was his only comment. They let the night draw an obscuring curtain across the turbulence of their minds.

Levi's life fell quickly into a routine. Throughout the week he and Charley worked daylight to dark, building the hide house and a smoke house. They cut and stacked hay and readied the traps for the coming season. Each night they fell into bed in total exhaustion, then rolled out at the first streaks of dawn to begin another day.

Each Saturday they quit at noon, cleaned up, and rode into town. Usually they took meat to sell, paying for their expenses with it. Charley spent every Saturday night and Sunday with Liz. Levi spent nearly every Sunday at the Millers. He fell into the habit of taking extra meat along, besides what they sold, to fill the Millers' larder, in return for all of their food he ate. It was becoming commonplace for Hattie to mention the name of some cowboy or some man from town who had obviously been visiting her as well. Each mention sparked a twinge of irritation in Levi, but Hattie never seemed to notice.

Every time either of them saw one of the Pucketts in town, he would quickly disappear, or walk away with a continuing glare laden with hatred. There was no attempt at confrontation, but the men's hate was so obvious and intense it was almost palpable in the air when one of them was near.

'What do you suppose is keeping them from taking a pot shot at us?' Levi asked Charley, as they watched one of the family slink away.

'The old man, I'm a-guessin',' was the response. 'He's older'n the hills, but tougher'n whang leather. He keeps them boys on a pretty short rope. He most likely tol' 'em to leave us alone, so they don't dare do otherwise, less'n they could do it so's he wouldn't be sure one o' his boys done it.'

Levi felt the skin crawl up the back of his neck with the thought that one old man alone was preventing an all-out attack by the entire clan. That cold wind up his spine told him that attack would come anyway.

NINE

'Fella on the ridge again,' Charley said quietly.

They were saddling their horses, just in front of the big lean-to they had erected as a livestock shelter. Levi continued the motion of saddling his horse, nudging the horse around enough he could look the way Charley's eyes rolled, without making his move obvious. It took him several minutes to spot what Charley had seen.

The early morning sun flashed once from some sort of metal in the trees at the top of the ridge west of the cabin. From a spot a hundred yards north two birds flew up abruptly a few minutes later.

'Movin' out,' Levi said.

'Headin' back north again,' Charley agreed. 'Somebody on one of them ridges 'most every day.'

'One o' the Pucketts?'

'I reckon. If'n they're gonna start somethin', I wish they'd get on with it. Sittin' here waitin' fer 'em is startin' to get on my nerves.'

'As long as we know they're around, they won't be apt to

catch us by surprise. I'm guessing they'll wait until they think we've forgotten all about them.'

'Sounds like 'em,' Charley agreed.

'Wonder if they're trying to see how close they can sneak without our hearing them,' Levi suggested.

Charley's head snapped up. 'Hadn't thought of that.'

'What say we set up a little surprise, to find out?'

'What d'ya got in mind?' Charley's eyes gleamed.

'Oh, maybe a few rawhide loop traps, that'll hang anybody up by the heels that steps in one.'

Charley gave a short laugh. 'Let's do it.'

They spent a day rigging a dozen traps in the timber behind the cabin. By nightfall they were satisfied they had protected every likely avenue of approach.

It was nearly midnight when a startled yell brought both men hurtling from their beds, gripping their pistols. They looked at each other, then broke into laughter.

'Reckon we'd oughta go see what sort of coyote we done caught ourselves,' Charley chortled.

Levi frowned. 'I'm not sure I want to go trotting out there in the dark,' he said slowly. 'There might be more than one. Besides, it might not hurt him a bit to dangle up there and consider the error of his ways for a few hours.'

Charley chewed on the idea for several minutes, then nodded. 'Sounds reasonable,' he said at last. 'I don't reckon either one of us is likely to sleep much though.'

At first light they walked quietly through the timber with guns drawn. The severed rope of the sprung trap dangled from the large, springy branch.

'Musta been right,' Charley said. 'Musta been two.'

Levi said nothing. He walked around the area, searching the ground carefully. Finally he straightened. 'Nope. Just one. Wearing moccasins, and leaving mighty little sign.

Quite a woodsman. He pulled himself up to where he could cut himself down. If he's one of the Pucketts, we got some good ones after us.'

In September, Levi and Charley began herding cattle into the valley from the surrounding hills. They branded both cows and calves that were unbranded, and hazed stock that was already branded out of the valley. They had put up a great quantity of hay – far more than either had thought they could. Haystacks dotted the floor of the vale in all directions. With the feed that was stacked, and the shelter the timbered areas provided, the dream of Charley's ranch was already well on its way to reality. By mid-October they had rounded up and branded nearly 200 head of stock, including five excellent young bulls.

Their smokehouse was filled with fish and meat, both smoked and sugar-cured. Charley had shown Levi how to slab the belly fat of bears, smoking it and making a bacon that rivaled pork when sliced and fried. It was still the only way Levi could tolerate the strong flavor of bear.

In late October, the first storm of the winter howled down from the high peaks. The temperature dropped forty degrees in less than two hours that afternoon. By dark the swirling snow blotted out everything. When the cold grey light of dawn filtered through the heavy clouds, the entire valley lay beneath a blanket of snow a foot and a half deep.

Levi and Charley rolled out of their blankets shivering. They finished a hurried breakfast, then set out, heavily laden with traps, stakes and bait. They returned twice for more traps and stakes. By dusk they had set out all the traps they could expect to maintain.

Unwilling to leave the traps untended to go to town, they began a changeless routine of a seven-day work week.

The winter was erratic for a month, then set in with a

vengeance. In the crisp bitter cold of every morning they set out each day to check their traps. They skinned the catches away from the cabin, often using the carcasses as bait for other traps, bringing only the hides to the cabin. Sometimes they also brought in the animal's brain, using it to tan those hides they wanted to retain for their own use.

A hide they kept, they scraped more carefully, then stretched and secured it on a frame. They took the brain and pulverized it, then placed it in just enough water to cover it. It was heated just enough to turn it a milky white. Then it was smeared over the inner surface of the hide and rubbed into the skin until it was all absorbed.

The hides were then stacked to allow chemical reactions that would preserve the hide and set the hair so they would not shed. Skins they wanted without hair were scraped on both sides before they were tanned. This way they prepared the deer hides from which they would make the buckskin shirts and trousers Charley was so fond of. Then it had to be pounded and rubbed to make it soft enough for wearing.

'Squaws chew it,' Levi said one evening, as he was laboring over a board-stiff piece of buckskin.

'What?' Charley said in confusion.

'Indians have their squaws chew the buckskin to make it soft,' he repeated. 'Ever seen them real soft white moccasins? They're elk hide that's been chewed until they get soft as silk. That's how they make the dresses they wear to get married in, too. Some of them dresses been chewed on for three, four months, to get 'em that soft an' white. Most beautiful things you'll ever see.'

'Now that'd be the real test of a wife, wouldn't it?' Charley grinned. 'I can just hear the parson! "Do you promise to love, honor, and chew this man's buckskin, as long as you both shall live?"'

'Or, "as long as your teeth hold out",' Levi offered.

Early winter offered ample opportunity for tanning. They made shirts and moccasins, and talked about everything they could think of to talk about. As the winter deepened, however, the catch in the traps got heavier, leaving less and less time and energy for anything but tending the prolifically producing trap lines.

'Ain't never seen the like,' Charley said one evening. 'Them pelts is the best I've ever seen, and I ain't seen an empty trap fer weeks. If'n this keeps up, we're gonna be the two richest trappers in Wyoming by spring!'

By late December it was no longer possible to go out without snowshoes. The first week they wore them, the muscles along the inside of Levi's thighs were so sore he could scarcely walk, but he conditioned to them quickly. Soon, walking with the spraddle-legged, swinging gait became second nature.

More and more Charley's conversations centered in his feelings about Liz. Levi grieved his own lost love but, as the winter wore on, at least some of those morose musings gave way to thoughts of Hattie, but he said little about it.

The occasional sightings of someone watching their valley from the ridges stopped as the snows got deep, and Levi began to relax.

He was nearing the end of the last trap line for the day, in late December, when he felt a strap loosen on his right snowshoe and bent forward to tighten it. As he bent forward, a bullet struck the tree behind where his head had been an instant before. Bits of bark showered him. Snow cascaded from the limbs of the tree.

As the echoes of the shot reverberated from the surrounding peaks, he hit the ground in a long dive and rolled behind a fallen log, nearly buried in the snow.

Keeping as low as possible, he slipped the strap of his .30.30 carbine from his shoulder. He eased his head up to try to see his attacker.

No sound broke the white stillness of the serene valley. Small animal sounds returned. Life among the wild resumed its routine, untouched by the nearness of death. No sudden flight of winter birds indicated any foreign presence. Levi studied the mark left on the tree by the bullet that had almost ended his life, trying to determine the direction from which it had come. Finally he decided it had been fired from the ridge of the valley, almost 300 yards away. Beside a clump of wild plum bushes near the crest of the ridge, he finally spotted disturbed snow. 'Came in on snowshoes to make a try,' he gritted.

Cold began to creep in through the gaps between his layers of clothing. His fingers and toes ached with cold. When nothing stirred for thirty minutes, Levi bunched his feet under him. He lunged from his cover and rolled behind a bush about three yards to his right. He gritted his teeth against the pain of the sudden exertion by his cramped muscles. No shots greeted him. He bounded in a long leap behind another dead-fall tree. Pausing only an instant, he jumped up and ran, zigzagging as fast as snowshoes would allow, from cover to cover, for nearly a hundred yards.

Satisfied, then, that his attacker had left, he worked his way cautiously up the slope to the cover from which the shot had been fired. The snowshoe tracks were there. Sign indicated the man had waited for at least an hour. A second trail led back the same way he had come.

'If there was daylight enough left, I'd back-track, and find out who wants to meet me so bad,' he muttered.

Instead, he returned to the load of furs he had dropped, resuming his course back to the cabin. That night he and

Charley discussed the near miss. They plotted ways to stagger their routine and increase their caution, to make themselves less likely targets.

When their chores were done, Levi collapsed into bed in the familiar nightly state of near exhaustion. That night, furtive movements in the trees and bushes crowded the face of Ann and the heartbreak she had given him almost entirely out of his dreams. His sleep was shadowed, instead, by the hovering, deadly spectre of unfinished business.

TEN

Wind-driven snow lashed the exposed part of Levi's face and he hunched deeper into the coat against its ferocity. 'If I'd known elk had busted a path to the next hay-stack, I'd sure never have made this trip,' he muttered.

He raised his head gratefully when he finally trudged into the shelter of the trees near the cabin, and gripped the stick on the end of the latch-thong between numbed hands to lift the bar from its brackets and open the door.

'Thought you said this valley didn't get so cold,' he grumbled at Charley as he began to shed layers of clothing.

Charley chuckled dryly. 'Think what it'd be up on top.'

'I'd rather not. It must be all of thirty below.'

'Cows OK?'

'Seem to be doin' fine. They're separated into two bunches, and both bunches can get to hay. Elk are eating as much as cows, but they're really earning their keep.'

'Yeah, this year,' Charley replied, 'but by next winter they'll be so many elk they won't be no hay left for cows. We'll have to fence off them stacks, somehow.'

'That'd take a pretty tall fence.'

'Ten feet or so, I reckon,' Charley agreed.

The weather turned bitterly cold the second week in January. The grip of the fierce weather continued for three weeks, then began to moderate. All the while the trap lines continued to yield a prolific harvest of furs. By late February the hide house was stacked completely full.

'We're just plumb outa room,' Charley marveled. 'Who'd a'thought that there hide house would be too small!'

'What do we do with furs now?' Levi asked.

Charley was silent for several minutes. 'Been thinkin' about that,' he mused. 'I reckon we gotta pull the traps. We can build ourselves a sled, maybe, and pull a load or two of furs into town on snowshoes. It's a long haul, but we'd get prime prices by gettin' the jump on everybody else.'

'It'd take us a week to pull a sled full of furs to Buffalo on foot, walkin' on snowshoes!'

'Yup. It's downhill most of the way, though.'

'Make more sense to use a big sleigh and the mules. We could bust a trail for them when we needed to.'

'Snow's five or six feet deep, most places!'

'I know that, but the wind's packed it so hard I bet the mules could walk right across it.'

'Think the horses could make it?'

'Sure.'

The next morning they began the job of removing all the traps. By night they were hung on the cabin, and there was a pile of furs that would not fit into the hide house.

The next day they dug out the buckboard, replacing the wheels with sled runners, and hitched the mules to it. The mules balked at the unaccustomed work. Charley's curses turned the air blue. His blacksnake persuaded them it was less painful to comply than resist. By nightfall they were pulling the empty sleigh easily across the top of the crusted snow.

They spent three more days breaking the trail down the valley with an empty sleigh. The mules began to condition. By the fourth day they were ready. They spent the late afternoon loading the sleigh with furs.

They rolled out of bed the next morning well before dawn, ate a hasty breakfast and hitched the mules to the loaded sleigh. Levi mounted his horse and led the way. Charley's saddled mount was tied behind the sleigh, and he rode the seat to drive the mules. The mules leaned into the harness and the heavy load reluctantly began to move.

Progress was surprisingly easy the first few miles, but slowed considerably when they began to break new trail. Two hours later Levi traded places with Charley, tying his horse behind the sleigh. When the animal had rested, they switched back again.

By mid-afternoon both horses and mules were worn out. They camped in a sheltered area beside a spring. 'Sure is something how springs run all winter,' Levi observed.

'Don't run very far,' Charley responded, nodding toward the cascades of ice stair-stepping down the slope.

The hobbled horses and mules foraged through the shelter of the trees for dried grass. Levi doled out a measure of oats to each. They built a small fire, cooked their supper, and spread their bedrolls on the ground.

'I left two furs apiece that ain't lashed down,' Levi said. 'Put them down first, then your bedroll on top.'

'Why not put them on top of me? That'd keep me warmer.'

Levi disagreed. 'You got plenty blankets for on top. The chill of the ground is what's hardest to keep away from. If

66

you get enough under you, you can always sleep warm.'

Charley took him at his word, and was surprised at how comfortably he slept. At first light they resumed the exhausting monotony of breaking a trail through the snow.

By mid-afternoon they came to the main road from Kaycee to Buffalo and camped again by warm springs that kept Clear Creek running all winter. They arrived in Buffalo shortly after noon the next day.

They went directly to the establishment marked with a sign 'Currier & Silverstein — Hides and Furs'. It took the remainder of the afternoon to sort, grade, count, and agree on a price for the load of hides. In the end, Abe Currier counted out just over $400, which Charley and Levi split evenly.

'That's a great deal of money,' the bespectacled merchant lectured. 'In fact, that's more money than I've ever paid for a single load of furs. The prices are higher than they have ever been. I wouldn't recommend carrying it around in this town. If the bank is closed I can ask Mr Arnold to open up so you can make a deposit.'

Levi and Charley looked at each other, agreed silently, and Levi spoke. 'We'd be much obliged.'

Thirty minutes later, with only what they thought they needed still in their pockets, the two left the bank. They went to the hotel, cleaned up, changed clothes, and Charley headed for the Pastime. Levi paced the frozen street for thirty minutes, then shrugged and headed for the Millers' house.

Even though it was the Millers' house, Hattie Nelson opened the door to Levi's knock. Her eyes lit up immediately when she saw him. 'Levi! I didn't expect to see you! I was afraid you would be snowed-in up there in the mountains until spring.'

The weight of winter lifted from Levi's shoulders as he basked in the brightness of her clear green eyes. 'We ran out of room. We rigged a sled and brought some furs in.'

'A sled?'

'Yeah, we made a bob-sled out of the buckboard.'

'Well come in!' Hattie said, remembering she hadn't invited him in yet. 'Have you had supper?'

Just then Becky Miller stepped into the front parlor.

'Well, Levi! You're just in time for supper. You will eat with us, won't you?'

'Evening, Mrs Miller. Why, yes, I'd be happy to.'

'I'll put a plate on. We don't have much company now that winter makes it so hard to get around. Even all the cowboys calling on Hattie have thinned out!'

Smiling impishly at Hattie's obvious embarrassment, she continued, 'All except that one young man from the J-Bar-Y. He seems to get here no matter how bad the weather is.'

Hattie quickly switched the conversation to the recent blizzard, and Becky allowed the matter to rest.

It was late when Levi returned to the hotel. He was almost to the stairway when he spotted Sheriff Angus. 'Top of the evenin' to you, Hill,' the sheriff growled.

'Sheriff,' Levi responded. 'How are things with Buffalo's upholder of law and justice?'

'Been pretty quiet, it has, for 'most the whole winter. Now that you've been findin' your way to town, I'm not so comfortable that it'll continue.'

'I sure didn't come looking for any trouble, if that's what you mean,' Levi protested.

'No, and I'm not sayin' that you are,' the sheriff agreed. 'I just thought you'd be needin' to know. Old man Puckett is poorly. It's sick in bed he's been for the whole winter. I'll be a surprised man if he sees green grass. It's him that's holdin' back those boys of his from tryin' to even up the score with you, so I thought you ought to be knowin', and watchin' your backside.'

Levi nodded thoughtfully. 'Thanks for the warning. I'm not sure they're going to wait. They've made a try three times during the winter. Got real close, once. Shot hit a tree right over my head.'

The sheriff's normally red face turned a shade darker.

'Did you see which one it was? It was one of the Pucketts, I'm supposin'.'

'I suppose so, but I have no way to know. I never got a look at them. The one that got snagged in a trap behind the house was a quite a woodsman, though. Wore moccasins and didn't leave any more sign than an Indian would.'

'That'd be Mordecai,' the sheriff responded. 'Tries to be like that Lewis Wenzel, he does. You know, the one they're tellin' all the stories about, from the old days. He is a deadly man, for sure. You snagged him in a trap?'

Levi nodded. 'We caught him, but it was dark so we waited till daylight. By then he'd cut himself down and was long gone. I saw a little sign of his slipping around after that, too, but he was watching for traps then, and never got caught in another one.'

It was the sheriff's turn to nod. 'Sure an' I'm bein' a surprised Irishman you caught him the first time. It must be he wasn't expectin' any kind of a trap.'

'You think the old man's about to die?'

'Sure, and it seems likely. If he does, you'd best be ready to fight off the bunch of them, I'm a-thinkin'.'

The talk drifted, then, to other things. Levi and Charley left at daybreak the next day, making it back to the cabin with the empty sleigh in one long day.

A week later they returned with another load of furs,

making the trip in two days. After that they made a trip a week until the hides were gone. By that time, Levi had more money in the bank than he'd ever owned in his life. 'I sure hope that fur trader knows what he's doing,' Charley growled. 'He's gonna be the sorriest critter in the country if'n them fur prices don't stay this high.'

During their last trip to town the sheriff sought out Levi again. Jacob Puckett, the rawhide-tough old man of the Puckett clan, had rallied and was gaining strength. With that, the threat from the Pucketts receded to that state of ready watchfulness that characterized all of Levi's life.

It was the little bit of relaxing that allowed Zach Puckett to spring his trap. It was his long-standing habit of caution that kept him from being totally successful.

Two weeks after the last of the furs were sold, the lowlands around Buffalo began to show sign of spring. The level of Clear Creek rose perceptibly, making it noisier than ever. The road turned to mud, making travel slow and difficult. The south wind bore melting temperatures, but it cut like a knife, making Levi and Charley hunker down into their coats as they rode out of Buffalo, heading south.

They had spent another weekend in town, and Charley was even more thoughtful than usual as they rode out. 'Levi, they's somethin' I got to ask you.'

Levi, his head ducked against the raw wind, glanced at the seriousness of his friend's face. Something caught movement out of the corner of his eye. He jerked his head around. A thousand lights exploded in his brain.

He was dimly aware of falling from his horse, and hearing the roar of anger from Charley mingled with the sound of rifle shots. It all swirled into a hopeless maze of sensations and sounds. He whirled ever downward into a deepening void, then there was nothing.

ELEVEN

Pain can be great. It means you're not dead. It was the first sensation Levi felt. Deep, throbbing pain began in the core of his brain, pounded its way up through harried nerve endings to explode through his skull with shattering force. He groaned and reached for his head. The world whirled in sickening spirals.

'Hold still, Levi,' a soft voice said. 'They're trying to clean the wound.'

He felt a hand grasp his. He gripped as though it would stop the wheeling circles of the room. Slowly the spinning subsided. His eyes opened painfully, then, slowly, began to focus. The doctor was working on the side of his head. Hattie Nelson sat gripping his hand.

'Where am I?' he moaned.

'Doc Winter's,' Charley responded. 'Zach Puckett didn't wait for the old man to die.'

'Where'd he go?' Levi asked, fear rising within him.

'To hell,' Charley said shortly. 'I got 'im.'

Levi closed his eyes. 'I caught a glimpse of him just

before he shot. Must have ducked, or else he just missed.'

'Just about missed,' Hattie corrected. 'I was just on my way up town when Charley rode in with you laid across your saddle. Oh, Levi, I was afraid you were dead!'

Levi felt a warm glow spread through him at the fervor of her emotion. It almost made him forget the fierce throbbing of his skull. If the doctor hadn't been plowing through the bullet's groove with what felt like a wire brush, perhaps he could have.

He was only dimly aware of being moved, of a soft bed, real sheets, and Hattie hovering over him. Levi thought, maybe it was worth getting shot.

Two weeks later they rode out of town again, heading back to the high valley. As they rode past the storefront of Currier & Silverstein, Hides and Furs, Charley spoke. 'Oh, say, that there reminds me. Whilst you was lyin' around with that headache, old man Currier stopped me one day. Seems he wanted to sell us back a bunch of our furs for just what he paid for 'em. Say'd he was havin' trouble shippin' 'em all. He reckoned as how we could freight 'em down to Kansas and turn a tidy profit.'

'Why would he want to give us a chance to do that, instead of doing it himself?' Levi responded thoughtfully.

'Well now, that's exactly what I was wonderin', so I started nosin' around. Seems we ain't the only ones got a bumper crop of furs this year. They's so many furs around the price done fell off somethin' awful. The crafty old coot was tryin' to get us to buy a bunch of ours back, and he knowed good and well we'd just get stuck with 'em.'

'I didn't suppose he'd do that,' Levi mused. 'Seemed an honest enough outfit when we sold.'

Charley chuckled. 'Most folks is honest if they's gonna make money doin' it.'

They rode for two hours in silence, then Levi suddenly remembered something. 'Say, Charley, wasn't you just asking me something when Zach tried to bushwhack us?'

'Wondered if you'd remember,' Charley responded.

'It took a while. Sorta got sidetracked, there, for a little while. What was it?'

'Well, I was wantin' you to tell me if I'm a fool.'

'For doin' what?'

'Well, I ain't done nothin' yet. Well, not official like, I ain't. But I, well, I guess I wanta get married!'

Levi pulled his horse to a sudden stop. 'Married? To who? The wh . . . to . . . to . . . .'

'Liz,' Charley supplied, with obvious irritation. 'Her name's Elizabeth, but she goes by Liz. An' don't you be callin' her a whore. She ain't no more. She's off the line, an' I been payin' her keep. I asked her to marry me.'

Levi started to respond several times, but caught himself each time. Finally he said, 'And did she accept?'

'She ain't give me no answer, yet,' Charley said glumly. 'She says she'd be plumb happy and proud an' all that to marry me, but she don't want to be married by no judge. She wants to get married in a church, by a preacher. Only she ain't sure a preacher'd do it.'

There was another period of silence. The melting snow was nearly gone close to Buffalo, but as they climbed higher it was deep and slushy, making travel slow and difficult. They gave full attention to the road until they reached another relatively clear area where they could ride side-by-side again.

'Did you ask the preacher in town?' Levi asked.

Charley shook his head. 'That was one of the things I wanted to ask you about. I know you go to church 'most every Sunday, if we're in town, so I figured you'd know the preacher. Fact is, I thought maybe you could ask him.'

'Why me?'

'Well, I don't want Betty there, if he says no.'

'Betty? Who's Betty?'

'Uh, well, that's Liz. That there's what she was called when she was a girl. That was afore her pa died an' her ma run off an' left her to fend for herself. Liz is sorta, well, that's the name she was usin' as a . . . a whore, an' I don't like it much. I been sorta callin' her Betty.'

'And if the preacher will do it, you actually plan to get married?'

Charley glowered. 'Yes, Mr Righteous Church-goin' Hill, we ax'shly plan to get married and build us a ranch, and have us a passel of kids. Is that all right with you?'

Levi was taken aback by the heat of emotion that boiled from Charley. They rode in silence while he turned over in his mind the things Charley had said about her, as well as the things Sheriff Angus had said about whores in general.

Finally he said, 'Well, I hadn't given it any thought before. I guess if you're sure, and you think she'll make you a good wife, then I'm all for it. You're the one that'll have to live with the fear that maybe, someday, the wild life will call again, and she'll go running back.'

'Aw, I ain't worried about that,' Charley protested. 'I know how much she hates what she's doin'. She just didn't know what else to do. If she marries me, I don't reckon she'd ever give whorin' another thought.'

'But what if you run into some of her old customers?'

'I guess maybe we'd just tell 'em she ain't on the line no more. Most cowpokes would just let it go at that.'

'And if they didn't?'

Charley shrugged. 'They would. Might take some of 'em a mite of persuadin', but they would.'

They rode in silence again for a good way. Then Levi said, 'When you plannin' on doing this?'

'Well, just pretty quick, if you could get the preacher to do it. If'n he won't, I guess we'll have to ride to a different town, or wait till one of them circuit riders comes through. The spring, for sure, though, either way.'

'You homesteadin' the valley?'

'Long time ago. I filed on the quarter where the house and the big spring are, and got the biggest fork of the crick in it, so's the homestead pretty well controls the water fer the whole valley.'

'I'll be needing to move my stuff out,' Levi observed.

'Well, now, we ain't wantin' to run you off,' Charley protested. 'We was thinkin' maybe you could homestead next to us, and we could work partners, fifty-fifty.'

Levi grew pensive. 'A few months ago that would've sounded awful good, Charley. I guess that's something I'd want a woman to share it with.'

'I been thinkin' 'bout that, too,' Charley enthused. 'I watched the way the widder Nelson was hangin' on to your hand and lookin' at you at the doc's. If'n you was to give her a little bit of encouragin', I'm bettin' we could just have us two families settlin' this here valley together!'

The idea caused waves of conflicting emotions to wash across Levi's mind. He said, 'I ain't ready for that, Charley. Not yet. I'll get my stuff packed up.'

'You'll talk to the preacher fer us?'

'I'll talk to him.'

Three weeks later happiness visited. The day was awash with sunshine. Flowers were beginning to bloom along the sheltered sides of houses. Charley, Elizabeth, Hattie Nelson, the Millers, Levi and a half dozen others gathered in the front of Buffalo's small church.

The mood was solemnly jubilant. The preacher talked of the joys of beginning a new life. He spoke at length about leaving old things behind. Then he read a service of marriage from a small, black book. There was total silence when he intoned, 'I now pronounce you man and wife.'

When nobody moved for several seconds, the preacher said, 'Well, kiss her!'

Charley awkwardly bent his head to meet her upturned and expectant lips. Silence continued for a heartbeat. Then a shout of celebration went up from the assembled friends.

The group paraded down the main street of Buffalo, whooping and hollering, all the way to the Millers' house, where a meal was waiting.

It was mid-afternoon when Charley and Elizabeth, riding a well-decorated wagon, clattered out of town heading south.

As Levi watched them out of town, he murmured, ' "The old things are passed away. Behold, I make all things new".'

Spring gave way to summer. Levi bummed around on various jobs. He rode for the T-Bar-A ranch during spring round-up, then rode shotgun for the Ten Sleep stage for a month while the regular shotgun guard was laid up with gout.

As soon as the last stage of that month was unloaded, he went to the hotel and cleaned up. Walking quickly, he went to the Millers' house to visit Hattie. He had been spending more and more time with her through late spring and summer. He delighted in her company, and had been thrilled as the sparkle returned to her eyes. Every week, it seemed, she grew pensive in memory of her late husband less often. Even so, the face of his own lost love kept intruding into his mind in all the unexpected and disconcerting times.

He was excited as he made his way to see her. He had seen almost nothing of her during the month he had been riding shotgun. He knocked on the Millers' door.

'Why, hello, Levi,' Becky Miller smiled warmly. Then a sudden cloud crossed her eyes. They flickered back to the interior of the house almost imperceptibly, and her smile became ever so slightly strained. 'Uh, well, uh, come in.'

'Is Hattie here?'

'Uh, yes. Yes, uh, she's here. Uh, come in.'

The skin crawled on the back of Levi's neck. He shifted his hat to his left hand. His right hand brushed the handle of his .45 and slipped the thong of the hammer. He eased the door clear open to be sure nobody was behind it, unable to explain the sudden change in Becky's attitude.

He stepped silently into the relative dimness of the house, willing his eyes to adjust quickly. The spotless appearance of Becky's house appeared normal. She had disappeared into the sitting-room, and he could hear the soft sound of voices. Nothing seemed alarming.

He stepped on into the doorway of the sitting-room and froze. Hattie was sitting in her favorite chair. Her flaming hair framed her face in exactly the picture that kept competing for space in his mind. Her brilliant green eyes were shining as she spoke.

Seated less than three feet in front of her a young cowboy was so rapt he hadn't even noticed Levi's entrance. Both of them spotted him at the same time. A soft sound escaped Hattie's lips, and she looked uncomfortable for just a moment. Then the look passed and she stood, smiling broadly at Levi. She walked quickly to him and held out her hands. As he awkwardly took her hands she spoke.

'Levi! I wasn't expecting you! You're OK aren't you?

Nothing happened to the stage, did it?'

'Uh, no. No, I'm fine. I'm all done with riding shotgun now. Shorty Macombe's back. I, uh, just thought I'd drop in and say "hi".'

'Oh, I'm so glad you did. I, uh, we haven't seen much of you lately. Uh, Levi, this is Skip Stoner. Skip, I'd like to have you meet Levi Hill.'

Stoner stood in an easy, fluid motion, extending his hand. 'Glad to meet you. I've heard a lot about you.'

Levi took the hand, impressed with the quick strength of the grip and openness of the young man's face. 'Stoner, pleased to meet you. You from around here?'

'Been in the country awhile,' the young man responded. 'Been ridin' for the J-Bar-Y.'

'That's up north, ain't it?'

'Uh, huh. West side of the valley. Real nice spread.'

'Good grass this year?'

'Real good. We already got more hay put up than we'll likely need all winter.'

As soon as he could without looking like he was running away, Levi prepared to leave.

'Oh, won't you stay for supper?' Hattie asked.

'Naw, I guess I'll ride on out to Charley and Betty's,' he replied, making his exit as hastily as possible.

He got his horse from the livery barn and rode quickly out of town, cursing himself silently. He camped in a small grove of trees at nightfall. He rolled out his bedroll, but never climbed into it. Instead, he continually paced the night away. In the dawn's light he saddled his horse and continued the ride to Charley's place.

As he rode into the yard Betty stepped into the doorway. Recognizing him, she waved brightly.

Levi had experienced a profound change in his attitude

toward Betty. It was difficult for him to visit with her at first, or to accept her as Charley's wife. As he spent time there, however, their love was too beautiful to deny. He watched the hard lines around her mouth disappear, replaced by laugh wrinkles at the corners of her eyes. The careless habits of Charley's bachelorhood gave way to courtesy and manners. Crude figures of speech were replaced by gentler terms. Some things simply were not mentioned. Seeing the transformation in both her and Charley, he had to admit their love was good and right and wholesome.

The change in the cabin was just as profound. Curtains hung at the windows. A checkered cloth graced the table. Subtle changes transformed the rude cabin into the coziness of a home. It emanated love, permanence and responsibility. It felt like a different world than it had been when only the two men lived there, and in fact it was.

As Levi watched the changes he felt many of them occurring in him as well. The transition from a lone wolf to a social creature felt good. He still spent long stretches alone, but no longer by choice. During each stretch he looked forward eagerly to his return to the company of Hattie and Millers, or Charley and Betty.

TWELVE

Levi frowned uneasily. Something about Main Street raised
warning hackles along his neck. He could see nothing out
of the ordinary, but the feeling persisted. He eased the
thong off the hammer of his Colt and rested his right hand
inches from it. His horse snuffled nervously.

People on the street seemed tense. Little knots of people
stood talking animatedly. An unusual number of horses
were tied up in front of the Big Horn Saloon. The town was
astir as if it was a Saturday afternoon, not a weekday.
There were too many wagons, too many horses tied up
along Main Street. There were too many people about.

He had been gone nearly two weeks. His visit to Charley
and Betty's place had been greatly helpful in sorting out his
ambivalent feelings toward Hattie. He knew he was still too
much stricken with his lost love to offer Hattie any
immediate plans. Even so, he felt a consuming jealousy of
Skip Stoner.

He thrust it from his mind now, tensed to learn the

reason for the unusual activity. He wheeled his horse across the street to the hitch rail in front of the sheriff's office. He dismounted thoughtfully, easing the gun in his holster, and walked into the sheriff's office.

Red Angus looked up as he entered. His eyebrows rose. 'Well, 'tis said if ye speak of the Devil he'll show up sure,' he rumbled.

'Town seems a little bit stirred up,' Levi responded.

'Cause to be,' the sheriff replied. ' 'Tis not every day we have to deal with something like this.'

'Like what?'

'You didn't hear?'

'Been out to Charley's. Just rode in.'

'Why were you stoppin' here, then?'

'Just thought I'd see what the stir was.'

It was the sheriff's turn to nod. ' 'Tis glad you did I am. I sent Skeeter Haasfeld out to Charley's to fetch you. You didn't see the lad?'

Levi shook his head again. 'I didn't follow the road all the way. Likely missed him. What's happened?'

'Jacob Puckett.'

'Finally died, huh?'

'Not by hisself.'

Levi's eyebrows shot up. 'Killed?'

'Ain't half of it.'

Puzzled, Levi waited in silence. The sheriff was obviously struggling for words. 'Died hard, he did. Everyone figured the old man was on his last legs, about to kick the bucket, but he held out a long time.'

'Held out? What'd he have to hold out for?'

The sheriff eyed Levi closely for a full minute, then leaned back. 'I'd best be startin' at the beginnin'. Seems everybody's always been knowin' that old Jacob had a wad of money stashed away. Talk is, he was everything from a road agent to a pirate in his day. He never even told any of his boys where the money was hid. Said he'd tell 'em, if he took the notion, before he cashed in his chips.'

'The rest of his family didn't even know?' Levi echoed incredulously.

'For sure not! You know that bunch! There ain't a one of 'em wouldn't kill all the rest for that much money. Now the boys has all been gone several days. They're bein' down to Cheyenne, gettin' some special bulls the old man had shipped out on the train from somewheres. Sent the whole kit and caboodle to be sure nothin' happened to them bulls.'

'They back yet?'

'Nope. Goin' to be hell to pay when they get back.'

'So who did it?'

'I'm gettin' to that. Don't rush me. Seems somebody knowed the boys was all gone. Whoever it was went out there, shot the Mexican cook, shot a half-breed woman old Jacob had for a housekeeper, and sorta persuaded the old man to tell him where the money was.'

'Persuaded him?'

A film passed across the sheriff's eyes. 'He'd have made an Indian proud, he would. Tied the old man down and used wires and rawhide strings on 'im. He put them wires and rawhide strings good and tight on all the places that'd do the most good. Guess he still wouldn't talk. Finally drug him outside and staked him out in an ant hill. Them big red ants. They'd make any man talk, they would, after a while.'

'You think he found the money?'

'Sure of it. The old man's bed was moved and the floor all tore up under it. There was a rock cellar right under his bed. Didn't have no entrance at all, without tearing up the floor. Nobody would've ever found it.'

Levi sifted the information through his mind slowly. Finally he said, 'You got any idea who did it?'

The sheriff shook his head. 'That's why I sent Skeeter out to fetch you. I thought, bein' sorta at loose ends, you might consider signin' on as an investigator. 'Tis quite a reputation you're havin' at that, you know.'

Levi let out a long slow breath as a dozen conflicting thoughts tumbled over each other in his mind. At last a dry grin began to play at the corners of his mouth. 'I do sorta miss it. What's the pay?'

'Eighty a month and ammunition. Spare horse if you need one. Livery barn bill on the county.'

'Fair enough.'

Fifteen minutes later Levi entered the street. The weight of the badge in his shirt pocket felt comfortable. The familiar words of being sworn in settled in his mind with the easy fit of an old memory. On impulse he turned down the Millers' street. Hattie answered the door. 'Oh, Levi,' she greeted. 'Come in! I was just thinking of you, and wishing you would stop by.'

'Shouldn't wish that hard,' he teased. 'Sorta like a lantern is with bugs. Just kinda draws 'em, you know.'

'In that case I'll wish all the time,' she tossed back with an impish tilt of her head.

He grinned foolishly without thinking of anything to say. After an awkward moment he said, 'You sure are all dressed up nice. You plannin' to go somewhere?'

Color left her face then returned a little stronger than it left. She cleared her throat. Her eyes focused on first one eye of his, then the other. She spoke hesitantly. 'I, uh, yes! Yes, I was getting ready to leave for a while. Uh, Skip asked me to go with him to try out a new buggy he just bought. Oh, I hope you don't mind. I, uh, he, that is I didn't know when you'd be here, and he did ask.'

Levi opened his mouth, then shut it, then opened it again to speak. 'I got no right to object. Why wouldn't it be all right? I got no claim on you.'

'But, Levi, I don't want you angry with me. If I'd known you were going to have free time and be here, I wouldn't have agreed.'

'I said it's OK,' he hurried too quickly. 'Bought a new buggy, did he?'

Her attitude changed with relief at the change of subject. 'I haven't seen it. He wouldn't tell me about it. He said he wanted to watch my face when I saw it.'

'Buggies cost quite a chunk of money.'

She nodded brightly. 'He's been waiting for some money that was owed to him. He was finally able to get it last week. He paid off his bill at the hotel and got a new saddle and another horse and the buggy. He bought me this dress, too. Do you like it?'

The muscles at the hinge of Levi's jaw bulged, but his face showed no expression. 'It's sure pretty, all right. So's the gal in it, for that matter.'

He was gratified by the pleased flush that hurried back to her cheeks, but the bunched muscles of his jaw did not relax. He was about to say something further, but was interrupted by an approaching man.

'Hill! Sheriff Angus sent me to fetch you. He'd like to talk to you, right away.'

Levi nodded wordlessly, offered Hattie a hasty goodbye, then wheeled off up the street. The sheriff was pacing the floor when he entered.

'Hill, I thought you ought to be knowin': the Pucketts is

back. Just heard they rode on to the place yesterday. They got the story from one of the neighbors. One of 'em came into town and talked around a bit. Nobody seems to be knowin' where they are now.'

'What do you think they'll do?'

'That bunch? Nothin'.'

'I might have a line on who mighta done it.'

The sheriff's eyebrows shot up. 'That quick? Who?'

Levi shook his head. 'Rather not say yet. Just found out a guy that's been needin' money awful bad just has all kinds of money, all of a sudden.'

The sheriff watched him closely, until it was obvious no further information was going to be offered, then he shrugged his shoulders. 'Don't you be forgettin', the Puckett boys are havin' a bone to pick with you, too.'

A sudden thought struck Levi and his eyes widened. 'I reckon I ought to ride out to Charley's first thing,' he said. 'Their feud is just as much with Charley as me.'

The sheriff nodded briskly. 'You do that. Then get back as soon's you can. This thing won't be takin' long to be blowin' the lid off the whole county.'

Levi could feel that lid already starting to move. He could feel it in the crawling sensation of death that crept up his spine. He hated that feeling. He also relied on it. It had never yet been wrong.

With great difficulty he waited till morning to set out. The sun was barely up when Levi got his horse from the livery barn. He rode at a brisk trot. It was nearly noon when he came into sight of Charley and Betty's place.

As he rode into the valley he stopped, as always, to drink in its beauty. The snow-capped mountains in the background, the multicolored forests of the hills, the green carpet of the meadows dotted with flaming wild flowers, never failed to send his heart soaring. He sighed heavily twice as he absorbed the most perfect of God's creation.

As he reluctantly took his eyes from the panoramic vista, he spotted the tracks of several horses he did not recognize. His brow furrowed. He looked nervously toward the house against its backdrop of trees. Nothing moved. There was no sign of life in or around the house that he could see. No smoke came from the chimney. He nudged his tired horse back into a trot, moving with an increasing sense of uneasiness.

As he rode within sound of the house he called out, 'Charley! Betty! Anybody home?'

There was no answer. His darting eyes took in the chewed-up yard. Horses had been around the house. Betty had designated the yard off-limits for horses. She had planted flowers, nurturing them tenderly. They were trampled into ruins. The door of the house stood open.

Sliding from his horse, Levi found his gun in his hand, as though of its own volition. He moved quickly to the wall of the house beside the door. He ducked his head into the opening and back as quickly as he could, then tried to digest what that instant glimpse had revealed.

His instinct recognized the scene before his conscious mind could digest it. His gun drooped to his side. As though in a dream he stepped into the room and stared.

Curtains still hung at the windows, giving an absurd air of normalcy and peace to the scene that assaulted his senses. Charley was nowhere to be seen. Elizabeth was all too readily seen.

She was on the floor. Each wrist was securely tied to a leg of the table. A dirty neckerchief was stuffed tightly into her mouth. She was totally naked. The torn remnants of her clothing were strewn about the room. Her legs were covered with blood. Her entire body was covered with massive bruises and welts.

Levi holstered his gun and dropped to his knees beside her. He jerked the neckerchief from her mouth, and saw with a flood of relief a flicker of response in her eyes.

'Betty! Betty! It's me – Levi. Can you hear me?'

For an instant there was no reaction, then, with an effort her glazed eyes began to move and to try to focus on him. He pulled the knife from its sheath at his belt and its blade slid through the ropes lashing her wrists to the table. He jerked the tablecloth off the table and covered her nakedness with it, then he lifted her head, cradling it in the crook of his elbow.

'Oh, Betty! Who did this? Tell me who did it, Betty!'

She tried, but only a croak issued from her throat.

'Just a minute. I'll get you a drink,' Levi said, laying her head back gently on the floor.

He rose to the water bucket on the wash stand, filled the dipper, and returned to her side. Lifting her shoulders and head, he held the edge of the dipper to her mouth and let a little of the water spill across her swollen lips.

She swallowed a little, then choked weakly. When she had cleared her throat she moved her head toward the dipper. She was able to drink a couple swallows before her head fell back against his supporting arm.

Levi let the dipper fall from his hands, spilling its water on the cabin floor unheeded. 'Where's Charley?'

'He's, he's hayin', up the valley,' she croaked with great difficulty.

Levi felt a rush of bitter relief that whoever had come here and committed this atrocity had not also killed his friend. 'Who did this?' he demanded again.

Her tortured eyes looked at him for a long time,

obviously trying without much success to focus on him. She swallowed laboriously, then whispered, 'Pucketts.'

A fire of hatred ignited in the pit of his stomach. It inched upward and outward as though it would engulf him with its fiery venom. His voice went flat and calm. He forced the white heat of his surging emotions to spiral downward into the icy prison of an emotionless void. 'Which ones?' he whispered.

'All six,' she choked, then coughed once, and a spume of bright red, frothy blood spewed out of her mouth. She tried twice to speak, but the blood welling up now in her throat made it impossible. Finally she was able to gasp out, 'They said, said they'd show that stinkin' hide-scraper once . . . '

She was interrupted by another gurgling cough that brought more of the bright froth. She swallowed desperately several times, then finished her sentence, '. . . once a whore, always a who . . . who . . . .'

She made a deep gurgling noise like a great volume of the bright spume was about to erupt, but it never came. Instead the gurgle retreated to silence. Her eyes glazed to a sightless stare.

With a terrible, detached calm, Levi lowered her head to the floor. He moved the tablecloth with which he had covered her nakedness to cover her face as well. He looked around for a piece of paper and pencil. He found both on a shelf beside the cupboard. He scratched a hasty note, hooked it on the outside of the latch-string of the door, then closed the door softly. The note stirred slightly in the breeze, bearing its warning message: *Charley. Don't go in. Pucketts came. Go get Sheriff Angus and the undertaker. I'll bring the Pucketts' bodies to town when I catch up with them.*

By the time Charley came in from the hay meadow, Levi was too far away to hear the howl of anguish that wailed across the quiet valley; that cry spoke all that could be said of unbearable pain, of a love that could not heed the warning of a scrawled note.

THIRTEEN

Levi rode in grim and detached silence. His emotions were bottled, sequestered into some remote part of himself. He sealed them away from any opportunity to interfere with the machine-like precision of a professional in pursuit of the business for which he was best suited. He was a hunter, totally engrossed in the hunt for the most dangerous game of all. Its culmination would be the death of the hunter or the hunted.

It mattered not at all that he was one against six. It held no significance that they must surely know they would be followed. It was of no importance the hunted would be savoring the certain approach of the hunter, and the chance it afforded to rid themselves of their greatest enemy.

For a year the Pucketts had nursed a grudge for Levi's incredible ability to shoot the brother he had killed. It would have been unforgivable, had he done so in a fair fight. It would have been only slightly less onerous for him to have done so from ambush. But it was worse than either alternative. He had shot Elijah, the fastest gun in the Puckett clan, as he had held twin guns on Levi, preparing to shoot him in cold blood.

That Elijah was no prophet. He had failed to read his own death in the face of the man he intended to kill. The gun had appeared in Levi's hand as if by magic. Elijah Puckett never even saw him move until he felt the bullet tear its way through his own chest. He died in utter bewilderment. Levi had made the fastest of the Pucketts look like an ignorant amateur.

To add insult to injury, both Levi and Charley had treated them as though they were no threat to their safety. The two had rigged humiliating traps in the timber around their cabin that gave no injury – only more belittling of the Pucketts' stature as men to be feared. Every attempt to frighten or harm Charley or Levi only succeeded in making themselves look foolish.

Then, when Zach ambushed the pair, he had only gotten himself killed. He had given the elusive pair no greater damage than one good headache, for which a second Puckett had paid with his life.

Now the seething hatred of the surviving six found an outlet as vile and despicable as they. They found a way not only to destroy Charley, but to do so in a way they could thoroughly relish. They had enjoyed, as only the completely depraved could enjoy, the endless rotation of six men repeatedly raping a woman tied in helpless submission.

They shouted and drank and reveled and assailed her with all the ribald and perverted humor of countless barrooms as each took their turn. They took sadistic delight in beating and whipping and poking and twisting to evoke responses from her battered body, even when she was beyond response. In the end, they left only because they were physically unable to keep it up any longer.

It did not matter that broken ribs had penetrated her lungs. It did not matter her spleen was ruptured. It did not matter she would likely die before her distraught husband would be able to extract the names of her attackers from her. He would know. He would come. Then they could finish their vendetta. When he was out of the way, they could go after the other one, and their quest would end.

The only flaw in their plan was that the wrong one of the pair found her first. He was not riding with the blind rage of a shattered husband. He rode instead with the cunning of a professional hunter of men, driven now by a cold fire of hatred that made him more deadly than any man they would ever face.

He was not racing in red heat of uncontrolled passion. His was the measured tread of the inexorable approach of the pale horseman of death.

Levi followed the trail of the six down the valley to the point where the hills were low and only sparsely timbered. He followed them when they turned off the road and crossed the ridge toward the valley in which the Puckett ranch was located. Each time the trail passed near any outcroppings of rock that would shield an ambush, he rode a circle around, keeping himself out of range of a sneak shot.

Each time the trail skirted the timber, he would ride back deeper into the timber, guessing the direction of the group's travel, then finding the trail when it broke into the open again. Twice he found evidence that one of the bunch had, in fact, waited in hiding for a time, then run his horse to catch up with the rest when the trap failed.

For three hours he followed the trail. He rode out on to the top of a low hogback and looked across the hollow in front of him. His well-trained eye could make out the trail of the six horses all the way across the hollow, disappearing into the timber on the far side. It was nearly a thousand yards across the hollow, so he could ride boldly more than half-way across. Then he would cut off at right angles and circle again. That way, if one of the group was hidden within the trees, waiting his approach, he would be forced to abandon the trap or take an impossibly long shot.

His eyes constantly scanned the edge of the distant timber for any hint of movement. He let his horse pick its way across the shallow valley. The thong was off the hammer of his .45, making it accessible to his lightning draw if needed. His .30.30 was across the saddle. His right hand held it with his finger on the trigger. He needed only to swing it and fire in one movement. With his left hand he held the reins loosely, letting them run under the rifle instead of across it, so they could not get tangled in the gun if he needed it quickly.

As he approached the half-way point crossing the hollow, he began to look to either side, seeking a point to swing toward, in his efforts to avoid an ambush. He was at the low point in the meadow. The lush grass reached to his horse's knees, muffling every step. The silence of the little haven from the world was complete.

He spotted the place he was looking for in the timber to his left. He tugged the reins to change the direction of his horse. Just as he did so, a shot rang out from the deep grass about fifty yards in front of him. He felt a blow to his midsection knock him backward from the saddle.

A searing pain ripped through his right side as he felt the ground slam against his back. For an instant that felt like a lifetime, he couldn't move. He gasped for breath and willed himself to roll over. As he did, he felt warmth spreading from the right side of his stomach. A wave of dizziness welled up within him. He fought it back down and forced himself to his hands and knees. He looked wildly about, gasping for breath, trying to force his eyes to focus.

As his vision began to clear, waves of pain radiated up from his abdomen. He steeled himself against it. He saw a shallow creek just to his right and crawled towards it as fast as he could make his body respond. Crawling into the rivulet of water he saw a shallow channel. It would let him crawl on hands and knees without the deep grass moving to constantly give away his position. As quickly and quietly as he could force himself to do so, he began to crawl upstream in the tiny creek.

As he began to crawl he heard a victorious whoop go up from the grass behind him. 'I got 'im boys! I blowed 'im outa the saddle afore he knowed what hit him!'

'You shore you got him?' a more distant voice shouted from the cover of the timber across the hollow.

' 'Course I'm shore,' the first shouted back. 'Mordecai Puckett don't miss no shots like that! Never thought o' me lyin' out in the grass fer 'im, the danged fool! Thought we'd stop in the timber instead. I tol' you it'd work!'

'You see him?' the other voice called back uneasily.

''Course I can't see 'im,' Mordecai responded. 'That grass is two feet tall. C'mon back and we'll pack 'im up and hang his body where the other one'll see 'im when he comes ridin' hell-bent after us.'

Levi kept crawling, fully aware that his time was limited before the alarm would go out, and they would begin to search on horseback for him. If he could reach the cover of the rocks and timber upstream before that, he could have a

94

chance to run or hide. If he was caught in the open, wounded and on foot, even he would have no chance.

As he crawled, he began to be aware of less grass and more rocks around him. He knew he was fast approaching the end of the cover of the tall grass. With relief he felt the course he was crawling turning to his left so he wouldn't be exposed in the bottom of a straight defile, open to his pursuers.

The rocks around him began to swim in dizzying circles. He collapsed to the ground, letting the wave of vertigo pass. As it did, the pain in his side forced his eyes downward. He saw the whole side of his shirt and pants painted bright red. With alarm he looked at the rocks he was lying against, and saw the tell-tale coloring that was like a road sign pointing his pursuers to his route of escape.

Alarm increased his adrenalin. He pushed himself into motion again. The rocks were bigger here. The brush along the sides was adequate to screen him from seeking eyes. He lurched to his feet. Just then the dreaded cry of alarm was sounded from the hollow behind him.

'He ain't here, Mordecai! Where'd you say he lit?'

'He's gotta be there! I blowed 'im clear outa the saddle. It's just high grass.'

A third voice chimed in. 'You plumb shore you hit 'im?'

'Spread out!' a new voice ordered. 'Zeke, you circle downhill. Ike, you circle the uphill side. Joe, you an' me'll ride back and forth through the middle. Mordecai, you keep your rifle ready. If he's just hurt and tryin' to hide, we'll spook 'im out.'

Levi stood carefully behind the shelter of a northern pine tree. He peered around its trunk, looking over the scene 200 yards below him. He watched the careful search work in circles around the horse he had been shot from. His hand instinctively dropped to his gun.

It was gone! Frantically, as though a second grab would change the emptiness, he slapped at his holster again. Empty!

'Here's his rifle!' a voice called. 'You musta hit 'im, or he wouldn't a' dropped 'is rifle.'

Levi leaned against the tree. A helpless emptiness filled him. It forced even the pounding urgency of his pain into a subdued level of awareness. For an instant, panic beat at his mind. He looked around in helpless fear for a way to flee. Even as he did, his long habit of calm clarity reasserted itself. He began to look for an avenue of flight that would maintain his concealment.

Shouldn'ta never ridden with the loop off my pistol, he chided himself silently as his eyes probed for a way of escape. Casting another hasty glance back at the group still scouring the bottom of the hollow, he ducked down and began a slow and silent flight from rock to bush, until he finally reached the relative momentary safety of a small stand of quaking aspen trees.

Moving as quickly as his wound would allow, Levi worked his way through the grove, then followed the scattering of brush and rock into the bottom of the hollow, following it as it went higher into the mountain defile.

'Hey! Here's his pistol! His gun done fell outa his holster. He ain't got no guns, boys!'

'Mordecai! You see which way he went?'

'I'm lookin'. Yeah! Here it is! Here's some blood on the grass. It looks like he's headin' up that way!'

'Be careful! He's still alive, and he might have another gun.'

'Spread out. Look sharp, and we'll just work our way in a line, so's he cain't get around behind us. We'll tree 'im or find him dead.'

Grimly, Levi knew the chances were overwhelming that the man was right.

FOURTEEN

Levi forced himself along the bottom of the hollow. Its sides steadily grew closer and higher. The way grew steeper.

The pain in his side sent waves of dizziness through him. His vision blurred with the exertion of his climb. He kept looking frantically for a place to hide, but saw nothing. His breath was ragged. Just ahead the ground seemed to top some kind of rise. He pushed doggedly forward.

The rivulet he was following turned into the spring from which it flowed. He looked quickly over his shoulder, then dropped to his knees and drank of the clear, ice-cold water.

He forced himself to his feet and crossed the ridge ahead quickly, moving far enough past it to keep from being silhouetted against the skyline. When he judged himself far enough, he stopped in the relative shelter of a clump of brush and surveyed his situation. A large hollow confronted him, backed by steep cliffs on all sides. The bottom of the hollow was thickly timbered with aspen and a few spruce. Rocks and brush bristled from the ground everywhere.

His eyes jumped to that wall of cliffs again, following its line slowly in a circle, clear around the hollow. There was no break in that wall anywhere. Frantically he started the circle back again, looking desperately for any feature that would indicate a crack in the cliffs. There was none. 'A box canyon!' he breathed. 'There ain't no way out! They got me boxed in here like a 'coon in a tree!'

He tried to quell the rising panic that rivaled the waves of pain and dizziness. He forced himself to walk again, moving down the slight incline into the hollow toward the dense stand of trees. He could hear his pursuers, just over the rise of ground that marked the edge of the hollow, as they shouted to each other. They had found enough of his trail to realize he had entered the box canyon. They knew there was no way out except past themselves. He couldn't make out their words, but the voices sounded like they were shouting in holiday spirits.

He reached the edge of the dense trees, and lunged into their cover only moments before the first eyes of the Pucketts peered across the rim. He pushed deeper into the stand, looking about for anything he could use as a weapon, or any place he could hide.

A deer trail afforded him a path into some of the thickest of the trees and brush. His eyes fell on a tree branch lying on the ground. It was about four feet long, and nearly three inches thick. It was part of a tree that had been in the path of an old pine, felled by some great wind. The shattered pieces of the tree lay all about.

Levi picked up the branch and hefted it thoughtfully, fingering the knife at his belt. He turned a complete circle, noting how sealed off this spot was from visibility in all directions. Only the deer trail offered any opportunity for a man on horseback to ride through.

He looked at the tangle of trees just beside the track and selected a spot against the far side of a standing tree. That tree gave him complete concealment from the direction he had come. The rise of the ground here placed his feet almost two feet above the deer trail. If he waited here, and one of the Pucketts rode down the trail, he would be invisible to him until he was right beside the tree. Then, maybe, if his side would let him move quickly enough, he could knock him from his saddle. Then, maybe, he could use his knife.

He leaned against the massive trunk of the great tree, fighting to control his ragged breathing. As he sucked in great gasps of air, he heard the approach of his pursuers.

'You shore he's here?' a voice asked, more softly than they had been shouting earlier.

'I'm shore,' the voice of Mordecai responded. 'I seen sign. I seen blood a time or two. He's either in these trees or in the rocks around the bottom of the cliff.'

'Let's spread out again,' the voice that was giving orders before commanded. 'Zeke, you stay up there on top, an' make shore he don't slip around and go back down. Ike, you an' Joe work them rocks around the bottom on foot. The rest o' us'll work through the trees. We'll snake 'im outa whatever hole he's crawled into.'

There was no more talk then. Occasional sounds rose of a horse stepping on dead twigs, or a leg brushing against a bush. Levi could hear scraping sounds in the distance, as Ike and Joe crawled across strewn boulders, looking in any crevice that might shield a man. It sounded like they were doing so boldly, certain by this time he had no weapon.

His breathing was nearly normal again, but his position against the tree was difficult to maintain. He kept flexing the muscles in his legs and arms to keep them from stiffening into uselessness, but was hampered by the need to remain motionless and silent. He caught his breath as he heard a slight sound.

It sounded like a horse had followed the deer trail into the small clearing and stopped. He had only heard that one small sound, but he was certain he was right. He knew the rider would be sitting still, prying his eyes into every bit of cover all around the clearing, being certain he did not ride past his quarry.

It seemed a lifetime later the bit ring clinked softly and the saddle creaked. Levi heard the horse's feet setting down softly in the loamy earth. He pressed back against the trunk of the great tree, willing the horse to make no reaction as his head passed the point of his concealment.

The sounds drew closer. Everything else receded to some faint and far away place. Noises of birds and animals, and even the other pursuers, were distant and unreal. The pain and pounding insistence of his own dizziness was pushed down. Levi's total concentration keyed on every step of that approaching horse.

The horse's nose came into sight, and Levi tensed. The next step brought the entire head of the horse beyond the tree trunk. His ears shot forward as he suddenly sensed the presence of the man lurking behind the tree. Knowing the rider would see that response of the horse as quickly as he, Levi lunged.

He stepped from behind the tree trunk. The club moved in a lightning arc, two feet above the saddle.

Simon Puckett saw his horse's ears spring forward. He jerked up the barrel of the rifle he held across his saddle. The gun barrel had risen only about four inches when a blur of motion crossed above it. Something smashed into his face. A thousand fragments of light exploded. Darkness engulfed him.

He was unconscious as he left the saddle. He never felt the startled panic that shot through his horse. He never saw the frightened animal lunge away from his falling body, kicking out in panic at the form his rolling eyes caught in motion at his side. He had no way to sense the hoof of that panicked horse as it penetrated his unconscious skull.

The force of the blow reverberated through Levi's body. The pain in his side blurred his vision. That blurred vision kept him from seeing clearly as the horse kicked the falling rider, then crashed off into the brush and timber, running wildly.

He shook his head to clear it. He raised the club to strike again. It was not necessary. Simon Puckett was dead.

'One down. Five left.' Even as he said it, Levi knew there was no way he could kill all five. A cry of alarm went up as Simon's horse broke into the clear. Levi grabbed Simon's pistol and dropped it into his holster. He slipped the rawhide thong over the hammer. 'Guess I oughta keep from losin' this one,' he muttered.

Picking up Simon's rifle he opened the breech, making sure it was loaded, then went through the man's pockets, disappointed at finding no extra ammunition. At his belt the dead man had a large knife. Levi took it, hanging it just behind his own. The detached part of his mind digested the sounds coming from the open space of the hollow.

'What happened?'

'He got Simon!'

'How'd he get Simon?'

'Aw, he didn't get 'im. That's that snaky horse that's always tryin' to stack 'im up. His horse just throwed 'im.'

'How d'ya know?'

'Didn't hear no shootin' did ya?'

'Zeke, track that horse back an' check it out.'

'Not me! That bastard's in there somewhere. 'Sides, I ain't no tracker. Let Mordecai do it.'

'Zeke, you yella-bellied polecat. You ain't worth the powder it'd take to shoot ya.'

As he listened, Levi kept looking for a different spot to wait for whoever came. He followed the trail of the fleeing horse until he could just see the body of the dead man. There, where the eyes of the searcher would be drawn to the body, he selected another spot of concealment. Again he began the painful wait.

The sounds of argument stopped. In fact, all sound stopped. A few insects buzzed in the air before him. Sweat ran down his face from the exertion of standing motionless. He forced his breath to remain slow and steady. His own knife was gripped in his right hand. He wanted no shots to bring the others down on him if he could avoid it.

It took a moment to realize the sounds of small animals and birds had stopped. Normal sounds of small creatures of the wild were unnaturally silent. If he had not recognized the warning of that silence, he would never have sensed the silent approach of the woodsman among the Pucketts.

Mordecai was good. His moccasins made no sound. Each step was careful enough to retract if a twig or branch was felt beneath the sole as it came down. Brush was carefully skirted. No tell-tale scrapes of sound gave his position. It was almost a sixth sense that allowed Levi to feel his approach and fix his position.

Just as that sense told him Mordecai was nearly beside him, Levi caught the movement of the man's hand coming into his line of vision. With a lunge as swift and silent as any move of which the woodsman was capable, Levi swept from behind the tree, his knife moving with blurring speed.

As he had hoped, the woodsman's eye had just caught sight of his fallen brother, and was momentarily distracted. A silent attack by knife was the last thing in his mind. If Levi had, in fact, killed his brother, then Levi would have guns. It was against a shot from across the clearing he was carefully guarding himself, not against a silent attack from right at his elbow.

For whatever reasons, his reaction was too slow. He caught the motion of his attacker in time to grab for his own gun, but the upward penetration of the knife blade below his rib cage stopped even that effort.

With stunned disbelief he looked into the haggard face of his attacker, even as he felt the point of the knife severing arteries and tearing its way through the muscle of his heart. His mouth opened wide in an effort to shout, to curse, to make some sound, but the searing pain and the rapidly approaching wall of blackness stifled the effort. He emitted one choked, gurgling gasp, and his knees buckled. Levi jerked the knife back as his left hand grabbed the woodsman's gun, pulling it clear of its holster as the man crumpled silently to the ground. He staggered backward until he felt the trunk of a tree behind him. He leaned back against it, letting his head settle against the rough texture of the bark, keeping his eyes carefully on the fallen man. He didn't move.

Levi hauled in great gulps of air, fighting away the encroaching waves of dizziness by sheer force of will. He heard groaning. He looked around for the source, then clamped his teeth as he realized it was him.

Pushing himself away from the tree, mechanically he wiped the knife blade on his pant leg, then replaced it in the sheath at his belt. He stumbled across the clearing, stepping into the protection of the trees at a point midway between where the two Pucketts had entered the circle in which their lives had ended.

Levi sank against a fallen tree. He was so tired! It didn't matter that he was about to die. It was of no consequence that he continued to bleed from the wound in his side. It was irrelevant that he was growing steadily weaker. It was unimportant that there were still four deadly Puckett brothers, who would very soon be stalking him again. He wanted only to sink to the soft ground and slide into the painless void of oblivion.

The log was so soft and comfortable. Even as he willed himself to alertness, he knew he could not win the battle. He felt the same dull resignation of death he had seen in Betty's eyes.

As he made that connection, he saw again the mutilated body of his friend's beloved bride. He began to feel again the burning embers of righteous anger burn within him. The adrenalin of his anger began to do what his force of will could not. His head lifted.

'Mordecai? Mordecai! You find 'im?'

The voice from outside the large copse stirred him from the stupor into which he was rapidly slipping. Levi shook his head and forced himself upright. The pain from the motion stabbed through him, but it served to clear his head.

'I tol' you he got Simon. Now he got Mordecai too.'

'Zeke, you an' Joe go around and come in the way Simon did. Me'n Ike'll follow in the way Mordecai did. Keep your guns out. He must be in there. We'll stay together, so's he can't sneak up on us. Let's get 'im.'

Levi forced himself to his feet. He checked Mordecai's gun that he still held, making sure its chambers were all loaded. Then he stuck it in his belt and drew Simon's gun from his holster, checking it as well. Suddenly he remembered Simon's rifle.

I left it standing against the tree by Mordecai! he cursed himself silently.

He switched Simon's pistol to his left hand and drew Mordecai's gun from his waistband, testing the balance of each gun. Holding one in each hand he stepped back to the edge of the clearing, just out of sight, but where he could watch both avenues of approach.

The remaining four Pucketts were men of deadly potency, but they were not woodsmen. Levi could follow the approach from both directions by the sounds of breaking twigs and clothes touching trees and brush. He could even hear an occasional grunt. He heard the gasps as the ones approaching from his left discovered the body of Mordecai. He heard them roll his body over to find the cause of death.

Just then the two approaching from the other direction almost tripped over the dead body of the other brother. One of them whispered hoarsely. 'Nathan! Ike! You there?'

'Shut up!' Ike whispered back, just as loudly.

Zeke ignored the command. 'We found Simon! He's dead. Looks like his horse kicked 'im in the head.'

'Watch!' the whispered voice of Ike returned. 'He's got Mordecai too! Stabbed 'im. He didn't even get a shot off.'

'Simon's guns is gone!' Zeke realized suddenly, forgetting the futile effort to whisper.

The four brothers walked toward each other, their eyes frantically probing the trees and brush around the clearing. They came together just across from where Levi waited. He knew he could wait no longer. He took one step forward. He planted his feet widely apart. Ike spotted him.

'There he is!' he cried as his gun swept around toward

Levi. The gun in Levi's right hand jumped and Ike grunted, his own shot passing wide of the mark as Levi's bullet slammed him off balance.

The clearing echoed then with a fusillade of shots from all directions. Bullets tore through trees and brush and the bodies of opposing men, tearing leaves and twigs and life away. A pall of gunsmoke rose above the sudden explosion of sound, and hung there.

Silence returned to the hidden clearing. The last of the men who faced each other crumpled to the ground. The pall of smoke drifted on a wayward breeze, ignoring the forms of seven men lying on the soft earth. There was no sound. There was no movement.

FIFTEEN

Eerie silence gripped the clearing. Dense trees twined their branches to hide the carnage from the world. Cliffs leaned forward to peer over the screening trees. Hollow stone eyes gaped in silent horror.

One of the prone figures stirred. He struggled to a sitting position. Guns in both hands lifted. He scanned the clearing for movement. There was none. As though by force of their weight, the guns sagged back to earth.

Minutes marched in silent lockstep. The man lifted the guns again. He slid one into the holster at his side and the other into his belt. He rolled to his hands and knees, stopped, head hanging, gasping with pain and exertion.

Slowly he heaved himself to his feet and stood swaying like a weed submerged in conflicting currents. His shirt and the right side of his pants were caked with blood, most of it dried to a deep brown. Red blood oozed from a groove along the left side of his neck. His left pant leg was soaked with blood from half-way between the ankle and knee. He felt gingerly to find the extent of the injury. 'Musta nicked me two or three times,' he muttered thickly.

He began to shuffle toward the deer trail. 'Gotta find a horse,' he groaned.

As he emerged from the trees, he saw two horses tied to a bush. He staggered to them, untying the one that shied least from the smell of blood. He forced his left foot upward until it reached the stirrup, tried to haul himself into the saddle. A tide of blackness engulfed him.

He opened his eyes, confused that he seemed to be lying on the ground. He squinted against the blurring of his vision. A horse stood above him, snorting nervously. Dimly he realized he was holding one rein. Groaning aloud, he rolled to his knees and hands. He grasped the stirrup for support, and hauled himself upright. He leaned, trembling, against the nervous animal.

Spotting a large rock jutting about a foot above the ground, he shuffled toward it, leading the horse. He positioned the horse beside the rock. Using the extra foot of height, he climbed laboriously into the saddle.

He lifted the reins. The skittish horse responded at once, walking with mincing steps toward the rim of the hollow and the trail that led back down the mountain.

Levi managed to stay in the saddle until the horse reached the rim and started the decline on its other side. As the horse began the downward course, the forward tilt of the saddle undid him. He fought for balance, grabbing for the saddle horn. A furrow creased his forehead as he tried to figure out how he could have missed it. He did not even feel himself land on the ground.

The horse's tolerance of this strange-acting rider was exhausted. He shied away, jerking the reins from the man's limp fingers, prancing sideways with mincing steps, tossing his head in fear and protest.

Levi groaned and tried to get to his feet, feeling fresh pain and bleeding from his wounds. He knew he had to find help quickly, but the idea didn't seem to excite him. All of life was removed from reality. Even the intensity of his pain seemed to belong to someone else, someone that he was observing from across some fog-shrouded valley. He didn't even realize he cried out in pain as he lurched upright.

The horse stood his ground as Levi approached. He let the man take hold of the reins. He sidled away, however, as he tried to reach the stirrup, and Levi nearly fell again.

After three more efforts, he managed to get his foot into the stirrup while standing on the uphill side of the horse, and hauled himself into the saddle. Swaying weakly, he felt the horse resume his course along the rivulet leading down the widening defile.

He felt himself swaying and knew he was about to fall off the horse again. Stubbornly, he grasped the saddle horn and tried to force the dimness from his mind. Faintly, he heard his name. It failed to register that he should respond. He heard the distant voice shout his name again.

The third time, the shout was closer, and he realized that he should stop the horse and respond in some way. He just couldn't do it. He willed himself to pull on the reins, to turn in the saddle, to call out in response to whoever was calling him. He got so far as to release the saddle horn to turn. The ground twisted upward in a dizzy whirl to slam against him.

Consciousness returned slowly. 'Hold still! I can't stop all this bleedin' if you won't hold still.'

Levi forced his eyes open. He realized, with a rush of relief, the face hovering over him was Charley's. He tried to speak, but only emitted a hoarse whisper.

'Ain't time to talk yet,' Charley said gruffly. 'I'll listen to you when I get this spot tied up.'

Trying desperately to remember where he was, Levi turned his head and saw tall grass all around him. His shirt was gone. So was the left leg of his pants. A wad of cloth was pressed against his lower right abdomen, held in place by a tight band made from his bloody shirt. Another band of cloth surrounded his torso a little higher. He frowned, unable to remember any wound to the chest.

Gingerly he felt the left side of his neck. A large glob of dried blood clung to his neck and shoulder, but he felt no fresh blood. Charley was binding a strip of cloth, torn from his own shirt apparently, around his lower left leg. When he had finished he nodded curtly.

'Now then, I guess we got all the holes plugged up. Now talk. Was it Pucketts?'

Behind the curt brusqueness of the big man, Levi could see a terrible fire burning. He winced as he remembered the cause, and marveled that he could keep himself in check.

'It was them,' he grated softly. 'All six of 'em. She was still alive when I got there. She told me.'

'She tell you why?'

'Didn't need to. She told me to tell you she loved you.'

Charley whirled abruptly a few steps, keeping his back to Levi. His shoulders heaved with the ferocity of his grief. It was several minutes before he could continue.

'You get 'em?'

'I got 'em.'

'All of 'em?'

'All of 'em.'

'How'd they get you? I found your horse, and the one o' theirs you was ridin', but that's all.'

'They're up above. They bushwhacked me. Mordecai was lyin' out in the grass. Never thought of him being there. He shot me outa the saddle before I even saw him. He thought I was dead, but I managed to crawl into a little draw and work up into the canyon.'

'Why'd you crawl off 'stead o' shootin'?'

'Lost my guns when he shot me off the horse.'

'Lost your guns?'

'Dropped my rifle, and my pistol fell outa my holster.'

'How'd you take 'em on, then?'

'Hid in the timber, where they had to split up to hunt me. Used a club on Simon. Used my knife on Mordecai. Then I had both of their pistols. It was enough.'

'Where they at?'

'Up over that rim. There's a hollow with a thick stand of aspens and pines and spruce. It's a box. There's a clearing about a third of the way in from this side. Follow the deer trail. They're all in the clearing.'

'Worry about them later,' Charley grunted. 'Got to go back and get the wagon to haul you to town. You ain't gonna make it, tryin' to ride.'

'Go make sure they're dead first.'

'They'll wait.'

'Do it now. I don't want one of them coming to, and walking up on me while I'm waiting.'

Charley thought about it for a little bit, then nodded in agreement. He mounted his horse and rode off at a brisk trot, up the bottom of the valley toward its upper rim.

Less than half an hour later Levi heard six slow, evenly spaced shots echo from the cliffs surrounding the upper section of the valley. He cursed silently and drew his gun, forcing himself upright so he could see past the tall grass.

His guns were both empty. Crawling to his horse, he used the stirrup to help himself stand, then pulled himself upright and reached into his saddle-bag. Grasping a handful of shells, he collapsed to the ground again, and began reloading one of the guns.

Finishing the loading of the gun, he kept it in his hand, holding himself up on his knees by grasping the stirrup. In a matter of minutes he saw Charley cross the rim and start the descent. With a gasp of relief, he allowed himself to pitch forward on to the ground.

He thought he had just hit the ground when he felt Charley's hands rolling him over on to his back. 'What are ya tryin' to do, get all the bleedin' started again?'

'I heard shots. Some of 'em still alive?'

'Nope. They're dead.'

'What were you shootin' then?'

'Just had to be sure.'

'You shot them again?'

He nodded grimly and swallowed twice. He swiped a sleeve across his eyes. 'One of 'em twitched when I kicked 'im, so I thought I'd make real sure.'

'You gonna come back and bury 'em?'

'Hell no, I ain't gonna bury 'em!' Charley exploded in what had become an uncharacteristic burst of profanity. 'Let the buzzards eat 'em. They don't deserve buryin'.'

Levi started to say something in response. He forgot what he was going to say. That cloud of darkness was back, sweeping across him with its numbing thickness. He felt himself float in to it.

He opened his eyes to the stab of pain that shot through his side. He groaned. 'Takin' it as easy as I can,' he heard Charley's voice from some faint, far away place.

His returning awareness felt the steady jostling of his whole body. It took several minutes to make a connection. Then he realized he was lying in the back of a wagon, moving slowly. 'Where we at?' he asked weakly.

'On the road just outside Buffalo,' Charley called back. 'Have you to the doc in half an hour now.'

'How long we been?'

'It's after midnight,' Charley said. 'Had to go back to the house for the wagon. I couldn't leave Betty like that, so I buried her afore I went back. Hope that was OK.'

Levi thought about it. 'Glad you did,' he tried to respond, but never knew whether he got it said.

He came to again to the feel of several hands lifting him from the wagon and carrying him inside. Then he felt the velvet folds of that merciful darkness again.

SIXTEEN

The sun stabbed painfully through squinted eyelids, its power plowing furrows into Levi's forehead. He lifted his hand to shield his eyes. It felt strangely heavy so he let it fall to the blanket.

'You're awake!'

He exerted a great effort to focus his eyes on the speaker. Hattie stood two steps from the window, where she had just opened the curtains. He tried to answer, but his mouth felt dry and stiff. He licked his lips. His tongue grated across them like sandpaper. He tried again, and a hoarse whisper came out, but its sound was unintelligible.

Hattie came to the bedside. She held a glass of water to his lips. He managed two swallows of the cool liquid before he choked. As he coughed, he felt a searing pain from half a dozen places at once, and a black cloud of dizziness threatened for a moment, then receded.

Memory came back with a rush. 'Where am I?' he asked. 'How'd I get here?'

'Lie back and be still,' she answered. 'You're at the

Millers', in my room. Charley brought you here, then got the doctor. You've been out most of the time for four days. We could barely manage to get you awake to drink a little.'

'Musta lost a lot of blood.'

'You did. The doctor said he didn't know how anyone could have that many holes in him and live.'

She started to say something more, but he was already asleep again. She bit her lip silently and set the glass of water back on the table.

Two weeks later the doctor allowed him to try to stand. He swayed slightly, his arm around Hattie's shoulders to steady himself. He had insisted on putting his own pants on before he tried to stand, and that had nearly exhausted him. Only his stubbornness kept him erect now.

He forced one foot in front of the other, intent on walking a complete circle around the room before he quit. One leg worked reluctantly well, but the other shot white stabs of pain through him with every movement.

'Legs musta got shot up some,' he observed hoarsely.

'Your leg and your stomach and your chest and your arm and your neck,' Hattie responded. 'Oh, Levi, why did you go after them by yourself?'

'A man's gotta do what a man's gotta do, Hattie.' The calm, strong voice of Skip Stoner spoke from the doorway.

Levi recognized the voice with irritation. He wanted to ask, 'What's he doing here?' but he didn't have the energy.

He hobbled the circle he set out for himself and eased himself down on to the bed. The room spun madly around him and he allowed himself to lie back on the bed for a moment before he answered. When he opened his eyes to try to answer her question, she was gone. He was lying on the bed, covered, and the sun was gone from the window.

From the other room he heard voices, talking softly. One

voice was Hattie's. It flowed across his mind like soft music. The other voice he thought was Stoner. Every time that voice spoke, he felt the rise of an inexplicable anger.

'Regular fixture around here,' he muttered.

The next day he tried again, with slightly greater success. The following day he was able to go to the table to eat with the rest. His expectations of that meal were abruptly shifted to a sinking disappointment when he saw that Stoner was there. He ate with wooden determination, hardly tasting the food, then returned to his bed.

As his strength began to return, so did his appetite. 'Gonna eat you folks outa house and home,' he commented.

'Takes a lot of food to replace all the blood you lost,' Tom replied.

'We'll expect a deer from you to replace it, when you're back on your feet,' Hattie said with a smile.

Tom snorted. 'Hnnh! Take more'n a deer, way he's eatin'! More like a buffalo!'

Levi smiled wanly, devoting his energy to swabbing the gravy from his plate with a piece of bread. Tom Miller poured some coffee from the cup into the high-sided saucer beneath it. Picking it up, he sipped the rapidly cooling liquid, watching Levi across the saucer rim as he did so. 'Have to admit, you're lookin' better every day,' he observed between sips.

Levi looked at Hattie. 'Where's Stoner today? First day he ain't had his feet under the table since I come to.'

Hattie looked uncomfortable, but Tom Miller only raised his eyebrows. A twinkle danced as he started to say something, then thought better of it.

'He went to look at some land up north, along Clear Creek,' Hattie offered.

It was Levi's turn to have his eyebrows lift. 'He has money to buy land, does he?' he asked, trying to be casual.

Hattie bit her lip, then seemed to make some silent decision. 'He's thinking of starting a ranch up there. He has money to buy a couple of homesteads that have good water rights. There's a lot of government range, and he has a few cattle already. He thinks that's the perfect country to ranch. It has the winter range along the river and summer range up in the mountains. We . . . he thinks the Heinlischer homestead would make a perfect home site for the ranch.'

Taken aback by her enthusiasm and the extent of plans that seemed to have been made, Levi fumbled for words. 'He must have come into a chunk of money,' he offered.

Tom noticed the undercurrent of his tone at once, but neither Hattie nor Becky seemed to. It was Becky who answered. 'He really did. He said his uncle had a big share in a silver mine or something down in Colorado. He got killed in a mine accident, and the other partner sold the mine to some big company. Skip was the only heir.'

'He tell you that?' Levi asked.

Becky nodded brightly, but Hattie's face clouded as she began to feel the suspicion in Levi's attitude. Becky said, 'He said he wished he had shown us the gold and the currency when he got here with it, but he was too anxious to get it over to the bank.'

'He put it in this bank?' Levi asked.

It was Hattie who answered, the tone of her voice beginning to sound defensive. 'He did after he cashed the bank draft at Casper. He said he had asked for the draft to be sent to Casper, because that's where he thought he would be. He was gone for several days after he got the letter that it was there. He got the money in gold and paper money and brought it up with him and put it in this bank.'

'Gold and paper both?'

Hattie looked uncomfortable. 'He didn't want it all in paper, but that much gold would be too heavy.'

'When was he gone?'

'He got back just the day you finished that last week of riding shotgun on the stage. You were here just after he was that day, remember?' Hattie asked.

'Anybody go with him?' Levi asked.

The direction of the questions finally led Becky to understand Levi's suspicions, and she gasped audibly. 'Levi Hill, you don't for one minute think that Skip had anything to do with the murder of that awful old man, do you?'

Levi was taken aback by the vehemence of her emotion. He shrugged. 'Just asking questions. It's my job.'

'Your job?' Hattie echoed.

'Uh, oh, yeah. I guess I didn't get around to tellin' you. I hired on as an investigator after old man Puckett got killed. Sheriff Angus hired me, and deputized me.'

Another thought struck him. 'You didn't find a badge in my clothes? It was in my shirt pocket.'

Becky and Hattie shook their heads together. Hattie said, 'Your shirt was torn into strips that Charley used for bandages.'

Levi thought about it for a moment, then shrugged.

'Musta lost it when I was crawlin' around over the mountain,' he said.

Suddenly realizing he was exhausted he excused himself and returned to his bed. Instead of sleep, he turned over too many strange coincidences in his mind. The timing, the amount of money, the mixture of gold and currency, all fit together like pieces of a puzzle. They all pointed straight to Skip Stoner.

When he finally drifted off, Levi slept fitfully. He swam in a long, delicious dream. He and his lost love were alone in a quiet aspen grove, in each other's arms. He awoke in confusion. Then reality swept over him. His mind reached desperately to grasp the retreating dream. It was gone. He felt it slip through the helpless tentacles of his mind with dismay.

Struggling from the bed, he went looking for Hattie.

'Where's my guns?' he asked abruptly.

'They're in the drawer of that bureau in the bedroom,' she replied. 'Why?'

'Just wondered,' he replied vaguely.

He walked as quickly as he could back to the bedroom and opened the bureau drawer. Strapping on the gunbelt, he checked the loads in his Colt. He drew the gun twice, surprised at its weight. A strange expression crossed his face. He drew the gun again, looking intently at it.

He saw Hattie standing in the door watching him. 'This is my own gun,' he said. 'How'd I get my own gun back?'

Hattie's face wore a flat expression he could not fathom. 'Charley brought it. He looked until he found it.'

'Where is Charley?' he asked, surprised he hadn't even thought of his friend.

'He's up in his valley, I think. Levi, he's drinking all the time. I don't think he's been sober since . . . .'

Levi pondered it for several minutes. 'Maybe I can ride up there in another week,' he said finally.

He left the house for the first time that day, walking slowly to the sheriff's office. He made it well, except when he had to walk in the unevenness of the road to get around the carpenters working on the building of Currier and Silverstein. They were installing a new façade, as well as adding on a large storage area in the rear. Once he got around that, he made it to the sheriff's office easily.

'Well, now, would you be looking at what the coyotes drug around,' Sheriff Angus said as he walked in the door.

Levi grinned weakly, sinking on to the closest chair.

'That's about what I feel like,' he admitted.

'What you look like too, if it's an honest appraisal you're wantin',' the sheriff grunted.

Levi ignored the barb. 'Anything new on the murder of old man Puckett?'

'Nary a thing,' the sheriff said. 'Just like the whole thing never happened.'

'What's happenin' with the old man's place?'

'The circuit judge had an ad put in the papers around lookin' for heirs, is about all.'

'Any show up?'

'One. Claims to be a son to the old man's sister. Winfield, his name is. He's livin' out at the place. He wants to sell off some cattle to get money to run the place on, but he can't till the judge decides whether it's his.'

'Got no money, huh?'

'Says not. Has a hundred-dollar saddle, brand new. Has a fine horse. Has a pair of matched, short-barreled Peacemaker Colts that'd fetch a fair piece of change, brand new. But he says he ain't got a nickel.'

'Doesn't quite add up. Where'd he come from?'

'Casper, he says.'

'When did he show up?'

'Three days after the old man was killed.'

Levi's eyebrows shot up and he pursed his lips. 'Quick. How'd he find out that quick?'

'Says he didn't. Says he just decided to come visit his uncle, and when he got there he was dead. Then you killed off all the Puckett boys, and he just fell into a ranch.'

Levi thought for a long moment. 'You know Skip Stoner?'

The sheriff looked at him carefully before he answered.

'I seen him around. Courtin' the same woman you are, according to the talk.'

The line of Levi's lips thinned perceptibly. 'Came back from Casper about the same day Winfield would have hit town. Came back with a whole wad of money.'

The sheriff said nothing, so he continued, 'Story he told was an uncle in Colorado left him half a silver mine. It was sold, and he got the money in a bank draft. The draft came to a Casper bank, so he got the money in gold and paper both and hauled it up here. He's been spendin' it pretty free.'

'Well, we're thinking down the same trail, looks like,' the sheriff responded. 'They rode in together, that day.'

Levi sat up straight abruptly. 'They know each other?'

The sheriff shook his head. 'They both say not. They say they just happened to bump into each other on the road, and sorta rode together for the company.'

They were both silent again for a time. 'What's Winfield look like?'

'A Puckett, only smaller and greasier and sneakier. I cannot talk to him without keeping one hand close to my gun and the other on my wallet. Nothin' he said, you understand. Real polite man. He just acts plumb sneaky. His eyes look like a fox eatin' a rabbit all the time.'

'Wanta hear a guess?'

'Just as well. I'm bettin' it'll match mine.'

Levi nodded. 'I'm bettin' they knew each other, all right. Because Winfield is kin, he knew the old man had money stashed, but didn't know where, of course. Stoner likely provided the brains and the imagination. He came to town and nosed around till he could find out a time the whole bunch would be gone a while. Then they rode in to visit dear old Uncle Jacob, shot the Mexican and the half-breed woman, then forced the old man to tell them where the money was. My guess is that Stoner got most of the money and Winfield got the ranch.'

The sheriff nodded. 'Only one thing wrong with that.'

'What?'

'The Pucketts. They couldn't know, when they killed the old man, that you'd kill all o' them. If they ain't all dead, one or all of them would inherit the ranch.'

'I thought of that. Their feud with Charley and me is pretty common knowledge.'

'It is that, but I'm not seein' how that fits the reasoning.'

'After the old man is killed, all they have to do . . . or all Winfield has to do . . . is bushwhack the Pucketts, one at a time, and it'll most likely be blamed on Charley or me.'

The sheriff's interest quickened. 'That's a good guess for a fact,' he reasoned. '"Tis a possibility to be sure.'

There was little more of substance to say, and the conversation lagged. Finally he rose. 'I'll work on it. If they did, I'll find a way to prove it. I think I'll wander down to the Pastime and listen awhile.'

SEVENTEEN

Levi was approached by the dirtiest man he had seen for a good while. 'You Hill?' the man asked.

He had developed a routine to build his strength. Each morning he would practise drawing his .45 until his arm grew tired. Then he walked to the sheriff's office and exchange news and guesses. Then he walked to the Pastime Saloon. He positioned himself at a table, his back to the wall, to watch the people who came and went. He gathered a pretty accurate picture of the town's activities and people.

The seventh day of his new routine, the man approached. He idly watched a greyback crawl through the man's hair as he answered. 'I'm Hill. What can I do for you?'

'Not a thing, my friend,' the man slurred. He reached one finger into his shirt collar and rubbed his neck. 'Just want to buy you a drink.'

'Why?'

'Favor you did the country, that's why. You're the one

killed off the Pucketts, ain't you?'

Levi's mouth tightened. 'So?'

'So you did us all a big favor. Them was the meanest, sneakiest pack of coyotes ever lived.'

'I take it you had trouble with them?' Levi probed.

'Not me. Nossir, not me. I stayed shy of 'em, I did. Even when they brung furs in, I always let one o' the others deal with 'em. I ain't gonna get myself shot, tryin' to do business with no Pucketts. No siree. They went an' dumped me in a horse trough once. Said I needed a bath. Scrubbed me with one o' them stiff brushes. Even then I didn't let 'em know I was mad. I just laughed like it was funny. They was bad 'uns, they was.'

'Didn't any of the horses die from drinkin' the water, did they?'

The man stared stupidly for several seconds. 'What d'ya mean?'

Levi shook his head. 'Never mind. Just thinkin'. You said furs. Do you buy furs?'

The dirty little man leaned closer. His breath nearly nauseated Levi. 'Don't recognize me, do you? I work for Currier and Silverstein. Leastways I work for them in the winter. I done checked out them furs you'n Johnson brung in last winter. First really big batch of the winter, it was.'

Slowly the man's face fit itself into Levi's memory. He remembered him among the employees of the fur traders.

'They don't offer much work in the summer, I don't suppose,' he offered.

'Nope,' the weasel slurred happily. 'An' I don't spend nothin' I can help all winter, then I don't have to work all summer. The others, they spend too much. Then they got to go find summer jobs herdin' sheep or fixin' corrals. Not me. I stay just as drunk as I can, all summer long, I do. Oh, in case you didn't notice, I'm drunk right now.'

'Really?' Levi said with artificial surprise. 'That must take a lot of money, to stay drunk all summer.'

'Not's much as you think,' the man bragged. 'I can stay drunk on almost nothin', if I don't eat much. Had to start late, this year, though.'

'Start late?' Levi invited.

'Yup. Trouble gettin' my money this year. They always pays me right when the work's done, but not this year. Waited till just about a month ago afore I got my money this year. I hate to stay sober that long! I was startin' to get right mad, I was, but they came through.'

'Be a shame if you had to stay sober all summer.'

The sarcasm bypassed the man's thought process completely. 'Oh, I was some worried about that, all right,' he agreed. 'I was some worried. But they came through. Old man Currier, he even gave me a five-dollar bonus!'

Levi quickly thought of several pressing matters that required his immediate attention, and left the man, surrounded by his own aura, sitting at the table.

Time passed quickly. Every day he spent hours practising the drawing of his pistol from every conceivable position. His normal speed had nearly returned. The gun still felt slightly heavier than it should, but he was confident his ability to draw and shoot was nearly restored.

As he was standing in the bedroom practising one day, he caught a glimpse of movement through the window out of the corner of his eye. Instinctively his gun leaped into his hand, covering the opening, but there was nothing there.

Carefully he walked a circle toward the window, watching closely. Nothing moved. When he was next to the window, he scanned the area revealed by its view, and saw nothing.

Frowning, he holstered his gun and walked outside. Passing around behind the house he walked to the area he thought he had glimpsed movement. Almost at once he found an area of grass, just behind a large tree, that had been trampled by somebody who had spent considerable time there. Cigarette butts littered the ground. A faint trail led from the tree into a shallow draw that extended a ways into town. The trail disappeared in the rocky bottom of the draw.

He scowled at the rocks as though to frighten them into revealing something more. 'Now who'd be slipping up here to watch the house?' he asked himself aloud.

Returning to the house he drew the curtains and left them closed. At supper he broached the subject. 'Any idea who'd be coming up behind the house to watch the room I been stayin' in?'

Alarm sprang to three faces. The seemingly ever-present Stoner only looked at him in open curiosity. The other three looked at each other, then back at Levi silently.

'I caught a glimpse of someone out my window,' he explained. 'I went out and looked. Somebody's been slipping up from the draw and standin' by that tree out back. Looks like he's been there for two or three days.'

Hattie suddenly got up and drew the curtains across the dining-room window. She stood beside them and faced Levi. Her face had lost its color. She was breathing as though she had just run. 'Do you think maybe that man related to the Pucketts is after you? Is that who you think it is?'

Her eyes leaped back and forth from Levi to Stoner, as though afraid of what his answer might be. Stoner only continued to watch in open curiosity. Levi could not fathom the man. He never appeared concerned or worried about Levi's suspicions. He made no real effort to defend himself or explain anything. He took everything with that open good nature, as though he had no care in the world. Either he was entirely innocent or one of those rare men who has no conscience, hence no nagging guilt to betray him.

He shrugged. 'I don't have any idea. I'll ride out first thing in the morning. If somebody's wantin' to make a feud out of my killing the Pucketts, I don't want him doin' it here. Besides, I got to find out what Charley's up to.'

Just after daylight the next morning Levi got his horse from the livery barn. He had the hostler bill the county for his keep and checked him over, pleased at his condition. He stopped at the bank and withdrew $50, then rode out of town. It felt good to be in the saddle again.

At the edge of town he caught a glimpse of movement from the edge of the draw where Elijah Puckett had lain in wait for him several months before. His gun leaped into his hand. He spurred his horse in an indirect line toward the spot.

There was nobody there. Fresh tracks revealed somebody had run his horse to reach the spot, then fled when he was spotted. Dust hung in the air along the bottom of the draw.

Levi holstered his gun and took in deep gulps of air.

'Wow!' he exclaimed to his horse. 'One burst of runnin' and I'm plumb out of breath! And you was doin' the runnin'!'

Turning the horse he returned to the road, but he rode carefully, certain he was being stalked by somebody. It was nearly dark when he rode up to the cabin that had been Charley's and Betty's home.

'Hey Charley! You home?' he called.

'Well I'll be danged,' a voice from within called back. 'I'd pert near give up on you ever straddlin' a horse long enough to get out here again! What'd they do, run outa venison in town?'

Levi grinned and slid off his horse. He nearly collapsed when his feet hit the ground, and he grabbed the saddle horn for support. 'Would you look at that?' he marveled. 'My legs won't even hold me up!'

Charley laughed. 'That's what you get fer lyin' around in a soft bed for weeks! Here, lemme put that there horse up. Git inside and sit yourself down, afore you fall down. By jing you look plumb peaked. Better'n you did last time I seen you, though.'

Levi staggered gratefully into the house and collapsed into the closest chair. He hadn't moved when Charley returned.

As Charley readied a lamp for lighting, Levi stirred. 'Why don't you pull the curtains before you light that,' he suggested.

Charley looked up quizzically. 'Why? You gettin' nervous in yore old age?'

Levi shook his head. 'Somebody's been slippin' up behind Miller's house to watch my window,' he explained. 'When I left town, he tried to get set ahead of me where Elijah did. I spotted him and scared him off, but I didn't see who it was. I thought maybe you'd know who it might be.'

Charley stood, match in hand beside the lamp, as though turned to stone. The match burned to his fingers. He let out a howl and threw it down, cursing. 'You get any kind of a look at 'im?'

Levi shook his head. 'Never saw anything either time except just a little blur of movement.'

Charley pulled the curtains across the windows and lit

the lamp. He threw together some supper, and they talked while they ate. When they were finished, Levi went wordlessly to the bunk that had been his before Charley and Betty married. He collapsed on it with great relief.

It dawned on him suddenly the bunk shouldn't have been there. He forced himself up to one elbow. 'You put the bunks back! What'd you do with the bed you made?'

Charley was silent for a long, painful moment. Gruffly he said, 'I burned it. Couldn't stand to have it here. Thought it might help to put the bunks back like they was.'

After a few minutes of awkward silence, Levi asked, 'You been hayin'?'

'Uh huh. I sorta hit the bottle purty hard for a while, I reckon. Then I decided hard work'd be a better way to get rid o' the hurt. Whiskey didn't make me forget her none. Made me forget everything else, but not how much it hurt to lose her. Anyway, I decided I'd best get to work, or I'd end up the town drunk. Hay's good this year.'

Levi started to answer, but it seemed like such an effort he wasn't sure it was worth it. Charley's last words faded off to some distant place. What was it he said about the town drunk? Oh well, it doesn't matter. The town drunk.

He remembered the town drunk. Now there was something, he thought sleepily. When he dies it'll take the undertaker two weeks to get his neck clean so he can lay him out. He wanted to laugh at the thought, but it took too much energy. He began to snore softly.

EIGHTEEN

The sun was high in the sky. Levi lay in the bunk for a while anyway, savoring the clean mountain air. Finally he dragged himself from the bed. Biscuits and bacon were still warm on the back of the stove. The pot of coffee was half full. He ate everything Charley had left for him.

Guessing which hayfield Charley would most likely be working, he found him in less than an hour. With the mules working a crude haystacker, he was intent on stacking the hay he had cut two days before.

'Got an extra pitchfork?' he called out.

'Not one little enough fer you to heft,' was the rejoinder Charley shouted in return.

'Aw, I oughta be able to kick it around on the stack for a while,' he protested.

With him in the stack and Charley loading hay on to the stacker to lift and dump on top, the two finished the stack in about three hours. Levi was exhausted.

'Lasted longer'n I figgered,' Charley observed.

'I'm weaker'n a pup!' Levi complained.

His strength returned quickly, though. Within the next two weeks Levi began to feel some semblance of his old self. By the end of that time he was working a full day.

They were just washing up for supper when they heard the hoofbeats of a running horse. Grabbing rifles, both men disappeared into the trees beside the cabin.

Levi lunged from his cover as Hattie appeared in the yard. Her horse was lathered and near collapse. She looked little better than her horse. 'Levi!' she called as she slid from her horse, nearly falling. 'Levi!'

'I'm right here,' he responded, running to her and grabbing her as she swayed on her feet. 'What's wrong?'

'Oh, Levi, I rode as hard as I could to get here. Levi, you've got to run! Now! Get your horse! Here's your money. I got it from the bank. Hurry!'

'Whoa, whoa!' Levi cut off the torrent of her words. 'What're you talking about? Go where?'

'Oh, anyplace! Anyplace! Just go! They're coming!'

'Who's coming? What're you talking about?'

'Jacob Puckett! Somebody thinks it's you who killed him. There's a posse coming.'

'Sheriff Angus thinks I killed old man Puckett?'

'No. Not him. He wouldn't deputize the posse. He tried to stop them. They waited till he was gone, then they all got their horses, and they're coming.'

'What made 'em decide I did it?'

'I don't know! Skip said it was the cousin of Puckett's. He's been trying to figure out a way to kill you. He's saying things to make people think you did it. Oh, Levi you've got to leave! They'll hang you, and you won't even have a chance to prove your innocence.'

'Could be she's right,' Charley observed. 'If they's a bunch lathered up fer a hangin', they ain't likely to think 'bout whether you done it till yore dead 'n cold.'

'I ain't much for running,' Levi said absently.

'Levi, you have to!' Hattie said. 'At least for a little while. Let things settle down. Then you can try to prove your innocence.'

'I got nowhere to go,' Levi said. 'My money's all in the bank . . . '

'No it's not!' Hattie interrupted. 'I persuaded Mr Arnold to give it to me. It's in my saddle bag.'

'He gave you my money?' Levi asked.

Abruptly Hattie seemed to remember something. Her face suffused with hot shades of red. 'I . . . I lied a little,' she stammered. 'I told him we had an understanding, and needed to go away together before the posse got here.'

'You told him we were running away together?'

'It . . . it was the only way he'd give me your money. I knew if you came back into town after it you'd be killed.'

'You told him we were going to get married?'

'I didn't say that, exactly. Levi, stop arguing with me! You've got to go! The posse can't be that far behind.'

Levi stared silently across the top of Hattie's head for a long moment. Finally he looked back at her. 'Stoner said he thought it was that cousin of Puckett's?'

She looked confused and reluctant to talk about anything except him running quickly. 'Yes, why? What difference does it make? You have to go!'

'Did he know you were riding out here?' Levi insisted.

'Yes,' she said with evident exasperation. 'Now will you please go?'

'Why didn't he ride to tell me?' Levi persisted in the line of questioning that was obviously frustrating her. 'Why did he let you ride all the way here, like that?'

'He said he was sure I'd be safe if I stayed ahead of them.

He said he'd follow them to be sure they didn't get here too quick. He thought they wouldn't even ride all the way tonight, but they might! I'm afraid they will!'

'I'll get you a fresh horse.'

'What are you going to do?'

'Go back to town. I ain't never run from nothin' in my life. I'm too old to start now.'

'Levi, don't! They'll kill you!'

'They may try.'

'Levi, listen. Listen! Levi, if you'll leave, I'll . . . I . . . I will go with you.'

'What?'

'I will, Levi. I don't want you to go back there. I'll go with you. We can go somewhere. This will all die down after a while. We can just start a new life somewhere. You have your money.'

The words spun in Levi's head. They sounded like an echo from a deep and painful memory. He almost sobbed. He took a deep breath while he got a firm grip on his emotions. He placed a hand on her shoulder. 'I can't do that, Ann. I . . . I mean, Hattie. I can't do that, Hattie. I think I could . . . I mean I don't . . . well, what about Stoner?'

'Skip? What do you mean?'

'It's been lookin' to me like things were gettin' pretty thick between you two.'

She reddened, but said nothing.

'Listen, Hattie. I guess I just ain't ready to love someone enough to ask you to run off with me. And I ain't never run from a fight. And I ain't never left anyplace with any kind of a cloud on my name. I'll be riding back to town with you, but we'll go my own way, away from the road.'

She looked at him for a long breathless moment, tears

streaming down her face. Finally she took a pair of saddle bags from her horse and handed them to him.

'Here's . . . here's your money. Oh, Levi be careful! You saved my life once. I've had to nurse you back from the dead twice. I don't want to bury you! You're the best friend I've ever had in my whole life!'

Gruffly Levi said, 'I'll catch you a fresh horse.'

When he had moved her saddle to a fresh horse from the corral, he saddled his own as well. She made a vain attempt to dry her tears and wipe their stains from her face. He threw the saddle bags she had brought behind his own saddle and helped her mount. Wordlessly he mounted and rode out of the yard, with Hattie close beside him.

The still hidden sun was just chasing the shadows into hiding as they reached Buffalo. Nothing moved in the street. Hattie swayed in the saddle. Levi's hand reached out to steady her, but his eyes kept scanning the street before them. They moved toward a shallow draw leading into town, avoiding the street.

They followed the draw to a large cottonwood tree. He dismounted stiffly. Hattie fell into his arms. He held her close while she wiggled her feet, trying to squirm life back into her legs. The soft scent of her hair and the feel of her body against him raised memories he thought too deeply stifled to surge so quickly to the surface. He tried to move away from her without allowing her to fall.

'We best get into the house,' he said gruffly.

She shot him a puzzled glance, then nodded. She staggered against the support of his arm for several steps, then began to walk more steadily.

The back door of the Millers' house opened soundlessly at his touch. Stepping inside he eased the door shut behind them, then motioned her back against the wall. He drew his gun, looking quickly around the kitchen, then spoke softly.

'Tom? Becky?'

'Who's there?' a sleepy voice responded.

'Everything OK?' Levi asked softly.

'What? Who's there? Levi? Is that you?'

'Yeah, it's me. Hattie's with me.'

Becky Miller swept out of their bedroom, drawing a robe around her long nightgown. 'Hattie! Are you all right? You look exhausted!'

'She's had a mighty long ride,' Levi explained. He turned to Tom. 'What's happening around town?'

'Nothin', now. There was quite a stir yesterday. That nephew of old man Puckett's got a bunch stirred up to go after you for killing the old man, but Sheriff Angus kinda broke it up. Then he tried again, and a half a dozen of 'em finally rode out. The shape they was in, they're most likely sleeping it off along the road somewheres.'

'The sheriff broke it up once?'

'Yeah. He made a little speech and told 'em to go home and go to bed or he'd let 'em sleep it off in jail. Murphy was drunk enough to get belligerent with him, and Angus rapped him alongside the head with his gun barrel. That kinda slowed the rest of 'em down. The only sober one in the bunch that finally rode out was the Puckett.'

'Winfield?'

'Yeah, I guess that's what his name is.'

Levi sifted the information through his mind for several minutes. 'Thanks, Tom. I'll take care of our horses, then I'll go talk to the sheriff.'

He went out of the back door, walking quickly in spite of his fatigue. He slid back down into the shallow draw on his heels and reached for the reins of their horses.

'Hold it right there, Hill!'

He froze in place, cursing his carelessness. He turned around slowly to face the voice.

'I figgered you'd be sneakin' in this way.'

The small, dirty man had a face that seemed to come to a point like a rat's. There was nothing rat-like about the hands, though, or the beautifully matched pair of short barreled Colt Peacemakers that stared unflinchingly at Levi's middle. He began to stall for time. 'You Winfield?'

'That's me. Did you really think you could kill off a whole clan of Pucketts and live to tell about it?'

Levi's mind was racing. He had drawn his gun in the house, in case someone was waiting. He hadn't holstered it until Becky came out of the bedroom. Had he slipped the thong back over the hammer? He couldn't remember!

'I got no quarrel with you,' he stalled. 'I don't even know you.'

'Well I got a quarrel with you! 'Course, I gotta thank you, too. It's thanks to you I got myself a nice ranch.'

He had to remember! If the thong was on the hammer, it would slow his draw too much to remove it. If the thong wasn't there, he might be able to draw and shoot before Winfield could react and shoot. He couldn't look. If he moved his hand to feel whether it was there, it would cause Winfield to shoot. He just had to remember!

'You don't look like the type that's cut out for ranching.'

The greasy little man gave a short, hard laugh. 'I ain't no dust-eatin', ground-sleepin' cowboy, for sure! But the man that owns the spread don't have to be a cowboy.'

'So what do you want with me?'

'Well now, I been thinkin' 'bout that. I just might let you walk away from here. It takes money to make money. Runnin' a ranch is gonna take a lot of money before it's time to sell calves. I want the old man's money. You tell me what you did with it, and I just might let you live.'

'What do you mean?'

'Don't give me the innocent act! You got to be the one who killed him and took his money. There ain't nobody else around here good enough to get past that old Mexican and tie the old man up both. That Mexican was one mean old gunman in his day.'

'I figured you had something to do with that.'

'What?'

'I had you figured for the one who did that.'

The conversation had gone on much too long. Levi could see the man's trigger finger tensing. Winfield would soon decide he didn't have the money, or else decide he wasn't going to tell him if he did. As soon as he was convinced of either one, he would shoot. He had to remember! He remembered sliding the gun back into the holster. Wait! Hattie had staggered a little just as he was holstering the gun. He had dropped the gun in its holster and reached for her. The thong wasn't on!

'Tell you what, mister tough range detective,' Winfield said. 'You did such a good job making that old man hurt till he told you where the money was, let's see how long you last. Now with a thumb and one finger, you slide that gun out and let it drop. Then get on that horse. We're going to get a ways from town and see how tough you really are.'

Levi lifted his left thumb toward his horse. 'You want the gun off my saddle first?'

For the barest instant, Winfield's eyes flitted to Levi's horse. The roar of Levi's .45 shattered the early morning stillness. Winfield took a step backward in stunned surprise. A second bullet took him back another step. The gun fell from his sagging left hand without firing. He tried to raise the right one to point to Levi, but it was too heavy, and it, too, fell into the dirt, discharging harmlessly into the ground as it struck. He looked down at his chest in confusion, then at the smoking gun in Levi's hand.

'How'd, how'd you . . . do . . . do . . . that?'

He collapsed forward on to his face. A sudden cloud of dust erupted from both sides of him as he hit the ground, then quickly settled again as he lay without moving. The sound of running feet came from the yard above him.

'What happened?' Tom Miller called as he reached the edge of the draw. 'You OK, Levi?'

'I'm fine,' he responded. 'Winfield thought he'd try to finish what the Pucketts couldn't.'

Becky Miller appeared beside her husband, then gasped at the sight of the dead man lying in the dust. 'Who is that?' she asked.

'Winfield,' Tom replied, putting his arm around her. 'He tried to kill Levi.'

Levi swung into the saddle. Taking up the reins of Hattie's horse he said, 'I'll send someone for the body.'

NINETEEN

The sun was barely up; it was too early to deal with death. Even so, he had killed a man: now he had to talk with Sheriff Angus.

He had decided it was either Winfield or Stoner who had killed the old man. Then he had decided it couldn't be Stoner. That left Winfield. Now it was back to Stoner.

He sighed wearily as he started up the street toward the sheriff's office. Already at this hour, the carpenters were busily working on the renovations of the Currier and Silverstein building, so he had to walk out around again.

He was half a block up the street when he stopped dead and stood there, hands on his hips, considering the beehive of activity on that building. He turned and walked on up to the sheriff's office. The sheriff was already at his desk.

'Mornin', Hill,' he said as Levi entered.

'Mornin', Sheriff,' he responded. 'I hear you bent your gun barrel last night.'

The face beneath the sheriff's flaming thatch of hair broke into a wry grin. 'Well, now, I haven't been checkin'' it, but maybe I oughta. Old Murphy has a hard head. Have you been meetin' that Winfield yet?'

Levi nodded. 'About a half-hour ago. He pulled down on me behind the Millers. I had to shoot him.'

'You shot him?'

'He had the drop on me. Said he was going to take me out of town a ways and see if he could make me tell him what I did with the old man's money.'

'Was he bein' serious now?'

'Seemed to be. He was hot about somebody stealing it.'

'Well, that must mean he ain't the one that done it. Are you havin' any new ideas, yet?'

'Maybe. What time's the bank open?'

'The bank?'

'I'd like to ask Mr Arnold a few questions.'

'Hank Arnold? Now you're not thinkin' he had anything to do with it, are you?'

'No. But he might be able to tell me some things that'd help. What time does he open?'

'He'll not be openin' for another two hours. He's always up early, though. We could be walkin' to his house.'

It was Sheriff Angus who knocked on the Arnolds' door. Lydia Arnold answered it at once, and smiled when she saw the sheriff. 'Well, Walter! Do come in. What brings you over this early in the morning?'

'Top of the mornin' to you Lydia,' the sheriff said easily. 'Lydia, this is Levi Hill. He's my deputy and a range detective. Levi, Lydia Arnold, purtiest lass in town. We'd like to be talkin' to Hank, if he ain't too busy.'

'Right out here, Red,' a voice called from the kitchen. 'Come on out and have a cup of coffee. I'm just finishing up my breakfast.'

They walked into the bright kitchen with its flowered

wallpaper. The table was covered with an oil cloth in matching colors. The cupboards were built right on to the walls, instead of the free-standing cupboards that most houses boasted. They stepped off the thick carpeting of the front room on to the shining wooden floor of the kitchen. Levi was impressed with the quiet elegance.

'What can I do for you this morning, Red?' Hank got right to the subject.

'Hank, this is Levi Hill. I 'spect you've been hearin' of him. He's got a couple questions to be askin'.'

'As long as you don't ask me how much money anybody has in the bank, I'll be happy to answer you,' he said.

Levi shifted uncomfortably. 'Well, that's pretty close to what I need to know. About a month and a half ago a young cowboy came into the bank with a large sum of money. His story is that it came as a bank draft to a Casper bank, and he withdrew it in cash to bring it here.'

'And what do you want to know about it?'

'Well, was it old money, or new money?'

'Meaning what?'

Levi hesitated, and Sheriff Angus spoke up. 'You can be on the level with Hank. Tell him what you're thinking.'

Levi nodded. 'Well, I need to know whether it was the kind of money he might have gotten from a bank in Casper, or whether it was more like the kind of money old man Puckett might have had hidden for a long while.'

Hank Arnold's eyes lit up. 'Ah, now I see what you're getting at. No, I think you have the wrong man. The money definitely came from a Casper bank. The bills were bundled, the way banks bundle them. Each bundle had a band around it. It was marked with how much was in it. The bank's identification was on each one. It was new money, as you called it. The gold coin was relatively new

142

as well.'

Levi sighed. 'OK. I thought that's what I'd find. Now the other question: one of the hands that works for Currier and Silverstein said they couldn't pay the help's wages in time, this spring. Fur prices really fell off. A little over a month ago, they paid everybody off and started remodeling the place. Did they borrow money from you?'

Arnold looked uncomfortable for a moment, visibly wrestling with whether, and how much, to tell them. Finally he sighed. 'Red, if this was anyone but you, I probably wouldn't tell this. No, they didn't borrow from me. The fact is, they owed me all I'd loan them. I was leaning on them a little, and I was honestly worried that I might have to foreclose on both their business and their homes. They both had their houses mortgaged, as well as the business.'

'Did have?' Levi led.

The banker nodded. 'A little over a month ago, Currier came in and paid off everything. He said they'd finally been able to collect for a big shipment of furs.'

'With gold?'

The banker nodded again. 'No paper money. Just gold. None of it newly minted. Some of it was awfully old.'

'Have you seen any old paper money around?'

Again Arnold thought before he answered. 'They've been paying the carpenters who work for them in cash. One of them brought a couple of the bills to the bank to exchange for newer ones. They're old and he wasn't sure they were legal tender. They were Union bills, but issued a good many years before the war.'

Levi nodded, his brow furrowed. 'But they were good?'

Arnold nodded. 'Perfectly good. Gold certificates, issued by the United States Government, printed in Philadelphia.

Perfectly good.'

Levi stood. 'Well, Mr Arnold, it was a pleasure to meet you. You too, Mrs Arnold. Thanks for your help.'

The banker obviously wanted to ask some questions of his own, but Levi did not afford him the opportunity.

At the door Mrs Arnold said, 'Walter, you stop over anytime, you and Cynthia. Mr Hill, it was a pleasure to meet you.'

As they walked away the sheriff said, 'How was it you've been puttin' that together about the fur traders?'

'Took a while,' Levi said. 'It was right in front of me, but I was too hung up on Stoner to see it. They tried to sell back part of the furs Charley and I trapped last winter, because the prices had dropped so bad. It just didn't fit together till I saw all the stuff they were doing to their store again.'

'You scout out the situation down there already?'

'No. I guess there's no time like the present, though.'

The sheriff nodded. Both he and Levi unconsciously slid the thongs off the hammers of their Colts, as they started down the street.

'Hill!'

Levi and the sheriff both whirled to face the unexpected voice. Skip Stoner stepped out of the front door of Rita's Café. 'You got a minute?'

Conflicting feelings chased each other through Levi's mind, but his face showed nothing. 'I reckon. What's on your mind?'

'I thought you might like to know, the bunch that rode out yesterday after you didn't get too far out of town.'

'How's that?'

'Well, they was all so drunk they couldn't hardly sit a horse. Half of them were asleep in the saddle by the time they'd gone a mile. By the time they got to Downing's

Grove, by the big draw, somebody decided they'd just as well rest in the shade for a while, and have another drink.'

'They all wanted to stop that quick?'

'All but Winfield. He tried his dangdest to keep 'em primed for trouble, but he had to pour too much liquor into 'em. Newt Graham fell off his horse and couldn't get back on, so the rest decided they couldn't go on either.'

'How do you know all that?'

'I was following them. I told Hattie I'd sidetrack 'em if they kept going long enough to get there.'

'Winfield stay there too?'

'No. He rode off back toward town, madder'n a wet hen. He's around somewhere, and he's sure got a bone on for you!'

'Yeah, well, thanks. You're a little late.'

'Why? He already try something?'

Levi nodded. 'Right after I got to town.'

Stoner's face blanched. 'Where's Hattie?'

'She's at the Millers'.'

'She OK?'

'She's fine. I rode back with her. Didn't seem quite manly to make her ride all that way alone.'

Stoner ignored the implication. 'What happened to Winfield?'

'I killed him.'

He digested the information, then nodded. 'OK. One more thing: I understand you been asking a lot of questions about me. Seems you think I might have something to do with killing the old man. I sent a telegram and asked for this. I'd take it kindly if you'd read it now.'

He handed Levi a piece of yellow paper marked 'Western Union' in large letters. Handwritten below the letterhead was a message:

'Arthur Stoner - stop - Buffalo Wyoming - stop - in response your request - stop - affirm bank draft received in amount ten thousand eight hundred forty-four dollars from Leadville Mining Co. Leadville Colorado - stop - withdrawn in cash by payee July ten past - stop - information also sent to Levi Hill Deputy Sheriff Johnson County Wyoming - stop - Stockmans National Bank Casper Wyoming - stop.'

Levi read it through twice, then handed it to the sheriff, who read it in silence, then passed it back to Stoner. It was the sheriff who spoke. 'You been for gettin' that wire, Hill?'

Levi shook his head. 'I sent for it the day I left town. Told the operator I'd stop in the next for an answer. I hadn't got back there yet.'

'You satisfied?' Stoner asked, his voice tinged with the first irritation Levi had seen the man express.

He nodded. 'Doin' my job, Stoner.'

'You could have asked me, instead of trying to make Hattie suspicious,' he insisted.

'You got intentions with her?'

'You bet! Honorable ones, I might add. You see, I always knew I was destined for more than a down-at-the-heels cowhand. I didn't know how, but I always knew someday I'd have a nice ranch and a good wife and a fine family. It's just meant to be. My ma, she always said that. I just had to wait for the time and the place, that's all.'

'You rode in with Winfield,' Levi stated abruptly.

Stoner was unfazed. He just nodded, matter-of-factly.

'Ran into him on the way back from Casper,' he explained. 'He didn't strike me as a man to be trusted, so I was careful not to let him know I had any money with me. That was easy. I hadn't spent any of it, and hadn't had a new pair of boots for two years, or anything else new, for that matter. It never occurred to him I was carrying money.'

'Good thing he didn't know. You'd have woke up dead.'

'Oh, could be. 'Course, I've knocked around some. I've been ridin' with the big boys for quite a while. He might have found it harder to get that money than you think.'

'Why didn't you get a bank draft? Been a lot safer.'

Stoner grinned. 'I hadn't never carried ten thousand dollars in my life. I just wanted to. Like I said, I figured I could take care of myself.'

Levi found, as always, the man's casual over-confidence wearing him thin. 'Must be nice to be so sure of yourself.'

Even the challenge did not faze the man's good nature.

'Just a matter of knowing my own ability. You have any other suspects in the old man's murder?'

Levi hesitated, then nodded curtly. 'We've got a handle on it. Matter of fact, we're about to see about it, so if that's all you wanted . . . .'

Grinning broadly, Stoner swept off his hat, bowed deeply in a parody of gallant forbearance, and strode off.

Levi took a deep breath. The sheriff spoke. 'Sure, now, an' that man could teach the Blarney Stone a thing or two about bein' glib, he could.'

'Sorta rubs a man's fur the wrong direction, don't he?' Levi agreed.

'Sure and he does that. But he seems a good open lad, for all that. I'm thinkin' he's just what he says he is.'

Levi nodded. 'Let's drop in and see how the fur business is coming.'

Even as he said it, that familiar cold wind crept up Levi's spine. Absently, he loosened his gun in its holster.

TWENTY

The headquarters and store front of Currier & Silverstein was the same beehive Levi had been forced to skirt the past couple of weeks. They wended their way through it, to the front door.

A thin, bespectacled man was perched on a high stool, poring over columns of figures in a ledger. He looked up as they entered. 'May I help you?' he asked.

'Is Abe Currier or Jules Silverstein here?'

'Mister Silverstein is not, but Mr Currier is in his office. May I ask the nature of your business?'

'Sure and you can ask where's the front door, you little skipjack,' the sheriff growled. 'You'd best be hightailin' out that door before I'm losing my patience.'

The little man looked momentarily offended, but something in the sheriff changed his mood. He grabbed a hat from the hat rack and scurried out of the front door.

Without knocking, both men walked into the office. Abe Currier looked up at once. His brows tilted toward his nose. 'Did you ever hear of knocking?' he growled.

The sheriff crossed the office to a position near the trader. Levi stayed across his desk, facing him. 'We'd like to ask you a few questions,' Levi said.

'What kind of questions? I paid you for your furs.'

'I see you're doing a lot of work on the place.'

'So? It's my business.'

'Where'd you get the money?'

'That too is my business. If this is an official visit, I might explain it. Over the past several years we have had increasing difficulty collecting our money from one of the wholesalers to whom we dispense furs. They were recently able to rectify their situation, so they paid us in full for a rather substantial back debt.'

'You got a name for that company?'

'What do you mean?'

'I'd like a name for that company. That way I can wire them and ask them to verify your story.'

'I will offer you no such thing! I don't have to defend myself to you.'

'I'm afraid you do,' Levi disagreed. 'We have evidence you murdered Jacob Puckett and stole his money.'

The fur trader's face blanched, but his expression of affronted dignity did not change. 'How dare you say such a thing! Get out of my office!'

''Fraid not, Currier. You see, the Pucketts had a cousin. One of the things he told us was that the old man had some money stashed with the rest that was special. The old man had collected some money from some government deal. He had one of the bills signed personally by President Jackson. It was a real keepsake. When a bill, signed by Andrew Jackson, showed up at the bank, we just naturally followed up on it. That bill was one you used to pay one of your carpenters.'

'That's a lie!' Currier yelled. 'There was absolutely nothing written on any of those bills!'

Recognizing what he had said, he stood, knocking over his chair. A double-barreled derringer appeared as if by magic in his hand. As it discharged, Sheriff Angus's gun barrel cracked sharply on his wrist. He howled in pain, and the bullet plowed into the floor.

'Sure and you're under arrest, Currier!' the sheriff said, shoving the man against the wall. He checked him for other weapons, pulling a Navy Colt revolver from beneath his shirt and a large knife from a sheath between his shoulders.

Levi said. 'Where's the rest of the money?'

Currier's eyes involuntarily darted to a safe across the room before he regained control. 'I don't know what you're talking about. There is no money. This is an outrage!'

'Open the safe,' the sheriff ordered.

'I can't,' Currier lied. 'Jules has the combination. I can't ever remember it.'

On a hunch, Levi grasped the handle and twisted. It opened easily and smoothly in his hand. 'That's all right,' he said dryly. 'I guess we can get by without it.'

From amongst the contents of the safe he removed four bundles, wrapped in oiled paper. Opening one of the packages, he held up a handful of bills. 'Looks like the rest of the old man's money,' he announced.

The resistance and belligerence went out of Currier like a punctured balloon. Wordlessly, the sheriff took him by the arm and shoved him toward the door. Levi followed, carrying the four packages of stolen currency.

As he stepped out he thought of the safe, its door gaping widely. Remembering the other money and books in it, he turned back to shut it. As he turned, slivers flew from the door jamb, showering him with wooden needles.

He dropped the packages of money and dived to the floor, rolling away from the door as he grabbed for his gun. He raised his head to look out of the window. He was immediately greeted with another shower of wood slivers from the window-sill. He jerked his hands up to protect himself from the cascade of broken glass tumbling all around him.

The glass stopped falling. He brushed it away to enable himself to move without being cut. Three more shots sounded from the same rifle, but he could not tell their target. None of the bullets entered the building. He gathered his feet under him, preparing to lunge across the room when he heard the sheriff.

'You hit, Hill?'

'No. I'm fine so far. You OK?'

'We're behind the horse trough. Sure an' every time I try to get a look, I'm gettin' a face full of slivers and dirt. You see him?'

'Not yet.'

'Are you havin' a professional plan for this situation, are you?'

Levi chuckled at the sheriff's dry humor. He answered, 'Yeah. Half a one, anyway. Stay put. I'll see if I can get out the back. Then I can circle around him.'

Eerie silence hung over the street. Levi kept his head down as he spoke. 'Was anybody workin' when you came out?' he asked the sheriff softly.

'Now that's a fine thing for me to miss!' the sheriff accused himself. 'There wasn't a man aboot when we came out, an' me missin' a thing like that!'

'Who's out there, Currier?' Levi demanded.

The captive fur dealer chuckled. 'Just Jules, and he's

more than a match for the two of you. He'll chew you both up and spit you out just like he did old man Puckett and that Mexican gunslinger of his.'

A dull 'thunk' was followed by a small grunt, then there was silence. Levi listened intently for a moment, then spoke. 'You OK, Red?'

'I'm better'n I was listenin' to that weasel.'

'What did you do?'

'Sure and I just laid my gun barrel against the side of his head. Tired of listenin' to 'im, I was.'

Levi chuckled dryly. 'You sure do like to bend that gun barrel of yours, don't you. Can you get where you can get off a shot or two?'

'Not without gettin' me shot up a mite, I can't.'

'OK. Sit tight.'

Levi left his position in a lunging dive that carried him beyond the shards of broken glass. He hit the floor rolling, as bullets dug furrows in the floor around him. Each time he hit and rolled he changed directions until he reached the door leading back into the storage area. As he lunged through it, he again dropped and rolled. Another gun barked suddenly from his right.

Leaping to his feet he whirled and saw a head and shoulder above a pile of lumber. He fired twice. The face disappeared behind a sudden shower of blood as the bullet and its accompanying shower of slivers riddled the face and throat of the gunman.

Levi crouched where he was, listening intently, but hearing nothing. Satisfied there was only one guarding the back door, he replaced his spent cartridges. He slipped out of the loading door of the fur warehouse.

He sprinted across the street and ducked between two buildings. Pressing against one of the buildings he waited.

There was no indication his presence was noticed.

Passing to the rear of the buildings, he began to run, moving in a large circle to come around behind whoever had the sheriff pinned down. When he had nearly completed the circle, he stopped to get his breath.

'Better wait a bit,' he instructed himself under his breath. 'Can't shoot straight when I'm out of breath.'

He was between the rear of two buildings, about three buildings from where he thought the shots had originated.

When his breathing returned to normal, he stepped away from the building. Gun ready, he began to walk softly in the direction the unseen gunman had to be hiding. He had heard no more shots since he emerged from the back of the warehouse. It was possible the gunman had fled.

He reached the opening between the next two buildings but hesitated to step into the opening. He backed against the wall of the store he was behind, then stuck his head into the space between the buildings, jerking it back before anyone there could react and shoot. There was no response. He repeated the move, but crouched down first, so his head would not be at the same level.

That time he left his head exposed an instant longer before jerking back, then digested the picture he had seen.

Finding nothing in the memory of that instant glance, he looked again. The area was empty.

He crossed the opening quickly, then repeated the tactic at the next two openings.

At the third opening he caught the shine of brass in the dirt near the front end of the opening. There was no longer anyone there. He stepped into the opening.

Just as he did, he felt his hat lifted from his head, even before he heard the shots behind him. The roar of a rifle blended almost exactly with the crack of a .45 followed instantly by two more quick shots from the .45. He whirled, dropping to the ground.

Near a clump of brush about fifty feet behind him, Skip Stoner stood with a smoking gun in his hand. Thirty feet to his right, Jules Silverstein was on his knees, looking stupidly at the young cowboy. As Levi watched, the dark-skinned fur dealer tilted sideways into the dust.

Stoner walked slowly to him and kicked the rifle out of his grasp, kicking it again to ensure it was out of reach. Then, cautiously, he removed the man's gun from its holster, keeping his own gun leveled at him as he did so. When he was satisfied he was disarmed, he stuck a toe of his foot under him and rolled him over. The dead man's eyes, focused at nothing, looked blankly into the sky. Satisfied, he holstered his gun and turned his attention to Levi.

'You OK, Hill?'

'A little nervous. Where'd you come from?'

'I heard the shooting, and saw the sheriff pinned down by the horse trough. I slipped around this way to see if I could figure out who had a bead on him. I didn't see anyone by the time I got here. I spotted you working your way around, so I hid in the weeds here to see if you needed any help. I almost didn't see him in time. He was hiding in the weeds too. When he stood up to shoot, I shot him. I got him quick enough to make him miss, but just barely.'

Levi fitted the information into his memory of the shots he had heard. It all dovetailed perfectly. He nodded.

Stoner noticed the reflection in Levi, and grinned.

'You just don't accept anything at face value, do you?'

Levi grinned in return. 'Just till I decide a man can be trusted,' he excused his suspicions. 'I'm obliged.'

'Well, you going to stand here all day, while the sheriff

lies in the dirt by that horse trough?'

'Well, might save the county some money.'

'How's that?'

'Well, there's Red's Irish temper, and Currier's tongue. If we leave 'em long enough Red'll drown him in that horse trough and save the county the expense of hangin'.'

Chuckling like old friends at the thought, they walked together toward the street.

'Will we see you again?'

Levi looked down at Hattie's face, and marveled again at the hypnotic beauty of her emerald eyes. 'Oh, most likely,' he said. 'I just might ride into that ranch up north there most any time, lookin' for a free meal.'

'Stick your feet under our table any time,' Stoner replied, standing close at Hattie's side proudly. 'You sure you won't stay for the wedding?'

'Naw. I might decide to steal the bride, if I did that,' he teased. 'I guess I'm headin' for Nebraska.'

'Nebraska?' Becky Miller gasped. 'That's so far away!'

'Oh, not too bad. I wired Pinkertons that I'd like to have my job back. Seems somebody over in Nebraska has been askin' for me to deal with some rustlers.'

Charley didn't say a word. It was evident he didn't trust himself to try to speak. He just held up a massive hand. Levi took it, gripping it wordlessly. Not trusting himself to say more, he lifted a hand and rode away.